The *Spirit* Catchers

The *Spirit* Catchers

An Encounter with Georgia O'Keeffe

KATHLEEN KUDLINSKI

WATSON-GUPTILL PUBLICATIONS/NEW YORK

ACKNOWLEDGMENTS

This book could not have been completed without the generous help of many experts. Eumie Imm-Stroukoff, librarian and archives manager of the Georgia O'Keeffe Museum in Santa Fe, showed me, among many other things, O'Keeffe's paintbrushes and color chips. Governor Everett F. Chase and Lt. Governor John Nieto of the Santo Domingo Pueblo in New Mexico read the manuscript for plausibility. The Pueblo artist D. Anguilar created the beautiful pottery bowls described in this book. Margarita Rodriguez corrected my clumsy Spanish. Jacqueline Ching and Laaren Brown at Watson-Guptill helped me catch (and edit) the spirit of my story. Wandering with me in the desert near Ghost Ranch, Hank and Betsy Kudlinski found the melting mountain, a cranky bat, the rusty windmill, and, finally, a wild rattlesnake.

Series Editor: Jacqueline Ching
Editor: Laaren Brown
Production Manager: Hector Campbell
Book Design: Jennifer Browne

First published in 2004 in the United States by Watson-Guptill Publications,
a division of VNU Business Media, Inc.,
770 Broadway, New York, NY 10003
www.wgpub.com

Front cover: Georgia O'Keeffe, *Ram's Skull with Brown Leaves*, 1936. Oil on linen, 30 x 36". Gift of M/M Donald Winston; M/M Samuel H. Marshall; M/M Frederick S. Winston. RMAC 1957.18.1 Photo by Richard Faller. Collection of the Roswell Museum and Art Center. Back cover: Portrait of Georgia O'Keeffe, New York, by Carl Van Vechten, June 5, 1936. Courtesy of the Library of Congress. Chapter art from *Ready-to-Use North American Indian Motifs* by Maggie Kate, Dover Publications, Inc.

Library of Congress Cataloging-in-Publication Data
Kudlinski, Kathleen V.
The spirit catchers : an encounter with Georgia O'Keeffe / by Kathleen Kudlinski.
p. cm — (Art encounters)
Summary: During the Great Depression, fifteen-year-old Parker finds himself homeless and traveling across New Mexico's desert, when a shepherd leads him to the artist Georgia O'Keeffe who teaches him photography and gives him a new perspective on life.
Includes biographical references.
ISBN 0-8230-0408-2 (hardcover) ISBN 0-8230-0412-0 (pbk.)
1. O'Keeffe, Georgia, 1887-1986—Juvenile fiction. [I. O'Keeffe, Georgia, 1887-1986—Fiction. 2. Artists—Fiction.
PZ7K9486su 2004
[fic]—dc22   2004003653

This book was set in Stempel Garamond.

Printed in the U.S.A.
First printing, 2004
1 2 3 4 5 6 7 8 9 / 11 10 09 08 07 06 05 04

To Susan Cohen
Yipee, Boss!

Contents

Preface

The aura of magic hangs over the harsh magnificence of the southwest desert. Dozens of Indian tribes' sacred places are there, and the world-famous artist Georgia O'Keeffe claimed to be "half-mad with love for the place" from the first time she saw New Mexico in the Great Depression of the early 1930s.

Those years following the collapse of the stock market and the United States economy in 1929 forced hard times on nearly everyone. Homeless and hungry, tens of thousands of desperately poor people wandered the roads or rode the rails, searching for work, any work. The crime rate soared, and bank robbers such as Bonnie and Clyde became dark folk heroes.

Things got even worse in 1931 as a record-breaking drought began to spread over three-quarters of the country. Dust storms blew up in the Great Plains, wherever overgrazing and overplowing had loosened the dry soil. The worst of the drought centered in the "Dust Bowl" states of Oklahoma, Texas, New Mexico, Colorado, and Kansas. Crops would not grow, livestock died, and suffocating drifts of dust buried entire farms. Thousands of families fled west toward imagined oases in California, bringing only the possessions they could fit in a car. Others pulled wagons. Still others just walked.

Yet not everyone suffered so badly during the Depression. Georgia O'Keeffe and other wealthy people still enjoyed comfortable lives and deluxe vacations. This book tells a story woven around O'Keeffe and a homeless teenager, Parker Ray, who stumbles out of the desert onto her doorstep.

The O'Keeffe of this book, her quirky personality, her ground-breaking modern paintings, and her techniques, are true to the year, as is the desert setting and the world history. Most of her quotes in this book are adapted directly from things she actually said during her long life. The painting, *Ram's Skull with Brown Leaves*, is on exhibit at the Roswell Museum in Roswell, New Mexico. The Ghost Ranch, now a spiritual center, is open to the public. Only O'Keeffe, her husband, the Ghost Ranch and its owners are drawn from life. The rest are entirely spirits of the author's creation.

After eight years, rain finally fell again in the Dust Bowl states, though the United States economy did not entirely recover until after World War II. In 1949, O'Keeffe settled in Abiquiu, New Mexico, where she lived until her death in 1986.

"When I think of death," she said, "I only regret that I will not be able to see this beautiful country any more—unless the Indians are right and my spirit will walk here after I'm gone."

CHAPTER ONE

Dust Boy

Parker looked over his shoulder and froze. A Model A crept slowly over the rise, glinting in the desert sun like a scavenger beetle. Goose bumps prickled the length of Parker's sunburned arms, but at least he finally knew what had been stalking him. He stooped to pick up a sharp rock, and glanced around. Patches of grass, cactus, and dry wind offered no shelter, so he lurched on down the dirt road, his boots as dry and cracked as his lips. Two days without water and he was almost ready to believe the lying shimmer of a mirage in the distance ahead. But there was no water there, he knew. There was no water anywhere. There never would be. After months on the road, he would die of thirst here in this desert. If thieves didn't get him first. Parker stopped, clenching the rock.

The Model A roared up behind him, then skidded to a halt in a cloud of grit. Sand stung Parker's eyes and dust covered his tongue with the familiar flavor of death. He tried to hack spit into his mouth to swallow, but he choked on sand instead. Coughing and gagging, he staggered off the road.

Ah-ooo-ga! the horn blasted. Startled, Parker gasped, sucking grit farther down his throat. He doubled over, fighting for breath.

The car door slammed, and Parker felt a hand slapping his back. He whipped around and raised the rock, ready to strike out if this one turned out to be like the others. Parker blinked. He could be looking at a face from a shaving-cream ad. Nobody, he thought, was really that handsome. Dark eyes, smooth skin, wavy hair. The stranger couldn't be older than twenty, but he had a face like a movie star's.

"Git your sorry carcass into the car, Dust Boy!" the young man said.

Parker coughed again and licked his lips, but his tongue was too dry to answer.

"Here you are," the stranger scolded, "staggering with the heat, maybe dying for water, and you can't take some help? You look half-starved, too. Now drop that foolish thing and git into the car." He smiled and winked. Parker grinned back and heard the rock clatter against others at the edge of the road.

"I'm Clyde," the stranger said.

"From Bonnie and Clyde?" Parker croaked. He took a step backward.

"Nah." The young man tipped his hat. "Though my girl would sure love that." He winked. "I'm Clyde Stebbins, hired hand from the Ghost Ranch up yonder." The impossible smile spread even wider. Parker felt his lip split as he grinned in response. "Where have you been, Dust Boy?" Clyde asked. "Bonnie and Clyde got themselves killed last year. A pity, too. Now get in, or die out here in the desert. Your choice."

Parker climbed into the automobile and sighed as he settled himself on the seat. "Water?" he whispered. He cleared his throat and tried again. "Got any water, sir?"

Clyde shifted into gear and propped his knee against the wheel to steady the car, then pulled a canteen from under the dashboard. "He'p yourself," he said, and grinned. "Not too much at first, now . . ." As Clyde eased the car out onto the road, Parker shook the canteen, savoring its weight and slosh. He meant only to sip, but his hands tilted the canteen skyward. Before he could gulp down the mouthful, he gagged, spitting the burning liquid across the dashboard and his own frayed blue shirt. Fumes stung his nose and made his eyes water.

Clyde roared with laughter and stepped on the gas. As the car lurched forward, Parker fought for breath. "What's the matter, Dust Boy? Never tasted whiskey before?"

"Let me out," Parker said, his throat burning.

"Oh, be a sport," Clyde pleaded, his voice warm and friendly. "I was just funnin' with ya."

Parker took a deep breath and shook his head to clear it of whiskey-stink.

"Where you headed?" Clyde asked.

"Home." Parker wished he could think straight. "Someday." He stared as Clyde pulled a six-shooter from a pile of rags on the front seat.

"Target practice, or maybe for varmint shootin'," Clyde explained, waving the gun in his left hand. "You ever been in a Model A before, Dust Boy?"

"Had one, back home—or did, until Pa had to sell it. Before he went off looking for work. Before the drought hit hard and the cattle all died." Parker's gut clenched around emptiness and the burn of whiskey. He made himself sit straighter against the frayed fabric seat cover. "Don't call me Dust Boy," he said. Then he added, "Please," and was sorry he had.

"Why not? Dusty hair and eyes and dressed in dust, head to toe, it's hard to see anything else about you."

"I been walking, looking for work since Black Sunday."

"You was in that killer dust storm last April? I bet that was wild!" Parker did not want to talk about it with Clyde. Or with anyone. "Wait now," Clyde said, "you mean to tell me you walked here clear from the Texas panhandle? You been on foot for four months?"

Almost half a year. Parker struggled with that thought.

"You lose anybody? Besides the cattle, I mean."

"My ma," Parker said, "and a little sister." Clyde whistled, long and low. "So," Parker went on, "you best not be callin' me Dust anything."

"You got some spirit to come out of that alive, boy," Clyde said. "Even if it don't show, right off."

Parker sat staring out as the desert whipped by, eating up miles of hot, dusty road—miles he would not have to walk. He felt dizzy with thirst and woozy from the heat and the bounce of the road and the firewater burning inside him. The car swerved and threw him against the door as a tire hit something solid. "What?" Parker grabbed for the door handle. Tires squealed as Clyde struggled to regain control of the speeding car.

Parker swiveled around to see what they had hit. A single desert tortoise lay squashed on the edge of the road. Parker replayed the short *thhop* sound they'd made as they hit the animal. He sat back against the seat, feeling sick.

"Hold on," Clyde said. He stepped on the brakes so hard that Parker's chin hit the dashboard. Parker blinked back tears and stared through the windshield. A herd of goatlike animals was crossing the road. They had long flowing white hair, all twisted and dirty. One called, *Baaaaa,* and another with widespread, pointed horns cantered to the lead.

"What's the matter, Dust Boy? You never seen Indian sheep?"

"Those are *woolies*?" Parker almost spit out the term. "Woolies are half the reason our cattle starved. Them and their mutton punchers, shooing the cattle from grazing the land."

"You want me to run down the shepherd for ya when he comes across the road?"

Parker decided to ignore that. "You sure they're woolies?"

"Churro sheep. Came to New Mexico with the Spanish." They watched the sheep meander across the road. *Ah-oooo-ga!* Clyde pressed the horn. Both boys laughed as the sheep skittered about frantically. "There's nothing so stupid as a sheep," Clyde said.

"Unless it's a sheep herder."

Clyde put the car into gear again. "So how old are you, Dust Boy?"

"Nineteen." Parker rubbed his soft sand-colored whiskers. He'd been lying so long about his age that it almost seemed true now. He looked out the back window. A tall, slender Indian boy rode into view on a pinto. Balanced across the horse's back, a lamb struggled weakly. The boy's dark eyes met Parker's and they locked gazes until the auto turned a corner and Clyde jerked the wheel to the side again.

Parker imagined the wet *pop* of another tortoise. When he had the car back under control, Clyde said, "I still can't square with the idea of you walking all those months."

"I worked a few days here and there." Explaining seemed like a lot of effort to Parker. He could hear his voice getting quieter. "Stayed two weeks at one place, till those folks had to give up, too. You're lucky to have a real job." He patted the cloth-covered seat. Last he'd heard, a new automobile like this cost almost five hundred dollars.

"This car isn't mine, Dust Boy. It belongs to the Ghost Ranch. That's a place where rich dudes come from back East to taste the real West." Clyde barked a laugh. "They got electricity half the time there, indoor plumbing, and fancy radios tuned to the Lone Ranger show at night. And they think *that* is the real West. Caviar and maid service, too." Parker shook his head in wonder.

"This Ghost Ranch . . . is it haunted?" He looked at the eerie rock towers looming over the road. "This whole place seems haunted. You feel it?"

"Some lady died long ago at the ranch, I guess. I never seen her, live or spook. But I have seen paychecks from there—and the name on them is *mine*," Clyde went on. "The ranch ain't hiring. Not nobody." Parker couldn't miss the warning in his voice.

"You might make out with one of those crazy Easterners, though," Clyde went on. "Or one of them foreigners. The guests are artists and writers, mostly. All loony, if you ask me, especially that O'Keeffe painter lady. You know how artists are."

"I don't. I never met one myself."

"Trust me, they're all crazy. But rich. They surely are rich. Especially that O'Keeffe."

Parker listened to his stomach growl. "So you think she's hiring?"

"Not so much hiring, as *having*, Dust Boy. I haul trunkloads of stuff for all the guests when they first come to the train station down in Taos. Then they get more shipped in by post. And they buy enough souvenirs from those Pueblo redskins to keep the whole tribe floating in cash. And they don't even lock their doors. . . ." Clyde laughed aloud.

"You saying I should *steal* from them?"

"Don't you get all high and mighty on me." Clyde stepped on the brakes and the car slid to a stop, kicking another cloud of grit and dust into the air. "It's hard times in this country," he said. "Depression times. You do what we all have to, to get by. Everyone does. It's only the crooks who are riding high. Bonnie and Clyde might of got themselves killed over in East Texas, but Ma Barker's boys and Pretty Boy Floyd are doing just fine, thank you. And take Dillinger. He just robbed the filthy rich."

"But those crooks killed people!" Parker was horrified.

"Only when some dang fool gets in their way," Clyde said. "Don't you tell me you never stole nothing. An apple off some farmer's tree when you was hungry? A pie cooling on a windowsill? A cool drink from somebody's well? A night of shelter in a barn?"

"That wasn't stealing," Parker shot back. "Not when I didn't eat for days. I only took what I needed. I'll repay it all someday." He stopped, realizing what he sounded like. "But I never did what was done to me, Clyde! My money was taken by road bandits. Pa's pocket watch. Ma's locket. And after that, when I had nothing, one of them just roughed me up for spite." He gestured at the string he'd knotted to hold his ripped shirt together.

"I wondered about that. You have nothing, you say? Nothing at *all*?" At the tone in Clyde's voice, Parker put his hand on the door handle to get away. The car jerked forward and he fell against the seat. "Show me what you got," Clyde demanded, his hand loose on the gun.

Parker pulled his pants pockets inside out and twisted to show Clyde.

The older boy snorted and pointed at Parker's chest with his gun. "You got something hid in there?"

Parker looked down at the paper peeking from his shirt pocket. "It's not cash," he said.

Clyde steered with his knees and reached out his hand, waiting. The tires shuddered on the rough dirt road. "Go ahead," Clyde encouraged him. "Jump out, then."

Parker looked at the boulders whipping by the side of the auto and pictured the squashed tortoises glistening in the sun. He pulled the photograph from his pocket and handed it to Clyde. The car slowed down as Clyde looked. "Pretty sad," he said. "These your folks?"

Parker closed his eyes, seeing them posed in a group at the farm. Sandy haired, all four of them. The farm in better days, with trees and flowers, soft grass and bales of fresh hay laid up in the barn. "That's the last picture I have of my pa," Parker said, "and all I have left of

Ma and Sally Belle." He hated the catch in his voice. "Give it back."
He grabbed after it, but Clyde jerked the wheel so the car swerved
hard to the left.

"Give it back! It's no good to you! Nobody would buy it."

"Nah," Clyde stepped on the brake. "I don't need it. I don't need
you, neither. Get out."

"Here?" Parker blinked. "But I'm thirsty." He heard his voice rise
like a little child's.

"Go, or I'll rip your picture to shreds." Clyde took the picture in
both hands and began to twist it.

Parker threw the door open and stepped out. "I have to head
over to town," Clyde said. He winked and handed Parker back
his picture. "Nice-looking folks. Hope you don't mind me funnin'
ya some."

"But I'm thirsty," Parker repeated stupidly. His head throbbed
and his tongue felt thick and slow.

"Oh, don't you worry yourself none." Clyde smiled widely, teeth
white and even. "This is just a short cut. The Ghost Ranch is right
up that dry wash. Follow it toward that funny flat mountain, the
Pedernal. Less than a mile and you'll see the windmill pump. It keeps
the horse trough below all full of cool, sweet water."

Parker stood, stunned.

"You had the gumption to walk for months, Dust Boy. A few
more minutes won't be too much now, right? Unless you're scared of
an old ghost or two."

"You were teasing me?" Parker asked. "With the gun, too?"

In answer, Clyde pointed the gun up toward the sky and pulled

the trigger. An empty *click* floated in the desert silence, and then
Clyde said, "Bang." He chuckled and said, "You didn't think I was
threatening you, did you? Me?" He shook his head and smiled his
movie-star smile again. "I always leave the first chamber empty so I
can spook folks."

A-ooo-ga, the horn sang, and then the Model A roared away.

Before the dust had settled, Parker felt it again. His watcher
was back.

CHAPTER TWO

Thirst

Clyde was gone. Parker took a deep breath and slowly scanned the desert around him. Sand-carved ridges ringed the valley, and the Sangre de Cristo Mountains loomed behind. Sharp-edged mesas poked into view. There were gullies, too, Parker knew, deep ones that might hide streams. Water. He ached for it. But where would he look?

Quick lizards darted across the hard-baked dirt near his feet. Above, the sky's blue blaze made Parker squint. Down near the hills, the sun and heat had bleached the sky itself white. An eagle soared low over the spare cactus tops, hunting.

Get going. Parker tried to concentrate on that thought. He had to find water, he knew. He would die without it. But just now, it didn't seem so important. Nothing did. Even the presence tracking him seemed only vaguely interesting. He shook his head to clear it and staggered.

When he regained his balance, Parker closed his eyes, listening for his pursuer. He heard only desert sounds: the dry rasp of cricket song, the rustle of wind through withered grass, the eagle's thin whistle, and then the dying scream of a jackrabbit. There was no crunch of footsteps. No branches snapped nearby, either, but the hairs on Parker's arms still bristled stiff with alarm.

A cat. Parker thought. A big one. That would explain the quiet. Parker tried to lick his lips. He couldn't just stand there out in the open if a cougar was stalking him. But where would he go? Parker shoved his hand into his pocket for his knife, then felt foolish. The bandit had taken it, along with everything else. The bandit before Clyde. Or was it Clyde? Parker felt confused. He wiggled his fingers inside his pocket, then pulled his hand out and stared at it. It was tingly and numb.

Move, something told Parker. He'd stood long enough in the hot sun. His thoughts were jumbled, but his need was clear. Water. "Follow the dry creek bed," someone had told him. Parker looked off down the road, then turned, fighting a wave of nausea, to look down the wash. *Move.*

"Well, shucks," he cussed aloud, making his decision. His voice sounded funny, so he swore again. His mama would be furious, he knew, but she wouldn't hear. She was somewhere else—ahead, maybe. Or was she dead? He couldn't remember. Parker stumbled down into the dry creek bed and sang her favorite hymn, "Faith of Our Fathers." It hurt his throat, but the words helped him focus. Singing had helped him walk for days, his legs swinging in time with the beat of the old melodies.

He grinned and felt his dry lips split. Parker tasted blood. "Listen to this, you old cat," he yelled at the cougar. "Ol' Susannah, now don't you cry for me!" He laughed aloud. "My singing would drive anybody away, wouldn't it, old boy?" He kept walking, belting out "Git Along, Little Dogies." Halfway through he changed it to "Git Along Little Kitty." Next he tried to sing "Jimmy crack corn and I don't care," but the words were all slurred.

"Wha—?" He doubled over laughing. He felt drunk! He staggered to the shade of a juniper bush and eased himself down on a big white rock. It took him three tries to prop his feet up on another rock. That one was reddish orange. Parker grinned again. He was as drunk as he'd ever seen Pa—or as delirious as his sister had been with a fever once.

Suddenly Parker struggled to sit up straighter. "I din' swaller Clyde's whiskey," he mumbled. "I can't be drunk." He struggled to understand, then yelled, "I'm dying of thirst! Water! I need water!"

Water. The echo came back at him. He turned quickly toward the echo and then had to wait until the scene stopped swaying. A cliff stood there, all colors and sunshine, and a windmill. It was rusty and still. Parker groaned. Now that he was not singing, the headache was back, worse than ever. His stomach felt sick, too. He pushed himself to his feet and staggered for balance.

"Wa'er . . .," he groaned, and stumbled on up the streambed to the watering trough at the base of the windmill. It was dust dry. When had he drunk his fill? he wondered. Two days ago? Three? He tried to remember the feel of water in his mouth. He pretended to swallow and gagged on his dry, swollen tongue instead.

"Justa' li'l farther," he told himself. "Clyde said . . ." He looked back over his shoulder to see how far he'd come, and lurched to his knees. When Parker looked back up the streambed, he yelped in surprise. A ram lay in the sand, staring at him, its eyes dark shadows.

Parker crawled to the ram, but it was only a skull, sun-bleached white and hollow. He reached out to feel its twisted horns, but his clumsy hands knocked the skull over. "Sorry," he slurred, and set the skull back up. He stared into its empty eye sockets. "Stupid sheep. You die of thirs'?" Parker felt like crying. "Me, too." He smoothed the fluffy white hair down the ram's muzzle and sighed. "Time f'r shome shut-eye." He leaned over and rested his head against the skull.

A clear thought surprised him. "You can' shut those eyes!" He backed away and stared into the eye sockets again.

This time, big moist eyes looked back into his, sheep's eyes with their strange sideways pupils. The ram blinked, its long white lashes feathering down and up again slowly.

"No, no!" Parker shook his head. He rubbed a wooden hand over his face. When he looked again, the sun glinted against dry white bone. Parker gave a half sob of relief. People *saw* things out in the desert. He knew that. Visions. But not him. Not now! You just need some water, the last rational part of his mind told him. Under Parker's arm, the skull shifted.

Parker jumped back and fell flat. The ram's skull had silky fur again and eyes. And it had a body, too. Parker stared as the buck struggled to its feet, stepped over daintily, and leaned close to his face. Parker felt the ram's feathery chin hairs, then its soft, moist nose. The ram's breath was warm on Parker's cheek, sweet and sage scented.

With his eyes closed, Parker imagined this was Ma, kissing him good-night in his bunk back home in Texas. He raised an arm and felt Ma's cheek, warm and smooth. But Ma wasn't woolly!

Parker stared into the ram's face and struggled to understand. It was too much work. His hand fell back onto the sand. This didn't have to make sense. It didn't matter. Nothing did.

Suddenly the ram straightened over him and snorted. Parker squinted at the horns, pale against the deep blue sky, growing, growing wide as a longhorn's, then wider still. A sharp hoof crashed into the sand beside Parker's head, once, twice, and then again. He rolled to the side. The ram was changing, looming ever higher into the blue. Its coat sparkled white in the sunlight, and its breath rumbled like thunder.

Parker heard his own heart beating, drumlike and fast. He tried not to see the vision—and he strained to take it all in. The ram reared up on two feet, now, tall as a cloud, snorting, staring, and shaking its horns. Parker followed the ram's gaze and locked eyes with a giant cougar. The ram snorted thunder again and twisted its head to drive a horn straight at the cat's eyes. The cougar spit and leaped out of the way.

"No," the ram roared distinctly. "No."

The cougar stood on its hind legs and roared back, whiskers glistening like the sun's rays. Parker's drumming heartbeat slowed almost to a standstill. He watched the cougar's paw swing in a great arc toward his chest. The ram's giant horns whistled downward, too.

The drumbeat stopped. Lightning sprayed as one sharp horn tip pierced the ground beside Parker's chest. The cat's paw smashed against the horn, its claws raking its length; but the ram held firm. "Not now!" it roared.

The cat yowled the sound of fierce wind. Its great tail lashed back and forth, tossing rocks in its way.

"Not now," the ram repeated. Parker flinched as the animal picked up its head slowly. It took a step over Parker, toward the cougar. The great cat hissed, spraying drops of spit onto Parker's face. The ram shook its antlers again, and the cat-thing bounded off.

Parker reached his tongue out to lick the cat's spit. It was salty, wet and good.

The ram leaned over Parker. "No," Parker gasped. "You're bleeding!" A giant cat's claw had torn through the ram's ear.

"Open your eyes," the ram told him. Its head came closer. The ram's torn ear dangled over his mouth. "What?" Parker managed to say. His eyes filled with tears as he realized what the animal offered.

"Drink." The ram's voice rumbled in the distance. A drop of blood splashed on Parker's lip, and he opened his mouth and drank.

There was no taste, only wet. Parker closed his eyes, slurping greedily. "Easy," the ram said. "There is plenty." Parker swallowed. With every sweet trickle, his swollen tongue softened.

The precious dripping stopped. "More," Parker gasped, and glared upward.

The large, dark eyes staring into his had round pupils, not bars. It was a person! Parker gasped and rolled to the side. "Let that settle." A strong hand held his shoulder. A hand, not a hoof. Parker struggled to understand.

"The ram?" he said. He looked into an Indian boy's face. He

knew this face! It was the shepherd from the road. A shepherd searching for lost woolies. "Was there a cougar?" Parker asked. He looked around quickly, then lay back. The Indian leaned over him again. "Did you see it?" Parker asked.

The boy slid his arm under Parker's neck and held up his head. Parker felt warm, strong, and safe. "Drink," the Indian said, holding a large pottery canteen to Parker's lips. Parker drank, then rested.

"Who are you?" Parker asked when he awoke.

"William Dark Sky," the boy said. Parker struggled to sit up and gestured toward William's canteen. In the background, a horse whinnied softly.

"What happened?" Parker asked after he had taken four or five cautious gulps. He handed the canteen back to William. "I saw . . . I saw . . ." He could go no further. None of it made sense—not the giant ram or the cougar, their colossal fight, or . . . He didn't even want to think about those very first sips. He shrugged uneasily and stared at the ram's skull lying on the sand. The tip of one antler was cracked and splintered, but the ram was dead. Long dead.

"You came close to the edge. I think you are seeing spirits."

"Spirits?" Parker laughed, then looked at the Indian. William wasn't even smiling. "You're serious?"

"Of course. Will you share some jerky with me?"

Parker nodded. His stomach had begun to feel empty, like normal. William tore a strip of dried meat in half; but before he handed a piece of it to Parker, he mumbled something like a prayer.

Parker hooted with laughter. "You just thanked the sheep for giving you his meat!" he said, and then repeated the joke. "You thanked a *sheep*!"

William did not laugh, but the jerky tasted delicious. So did the last swallow of water before he got to his feet and offered Parker a hand. "Think you can ride?"

Parker was beginning to feel normal again, normal enough to know that this William was very strange. Parker made it to his feet without touching the Indian's hand. The kid was spooky, he thought, but then all Indians were.

"How did you find me?" he asked.

"I am a shepherd," William said. "I am one with the sheep in the desert."

"You're pulling my leg."

William silently gathered the wool blanket that had been folded into a pillow under Parker's head. He slung the blanket and the heavy canteen over his shoulder and walked toward the horse. When Parker tried to follow, he lost his balance and sank to his knees. The Indian did not seem to notice but calmly led his pinto back.

Reins dangled near his face and Parker looked up at the horse. She was bareback and rangy. From the ground, the mare looked far taller than the ram had at first. The memory of that vision soared into the sky in Parker's mind, glittering in the sunshine and rumbling like thunder.

"You need to rest out of the sun," William said, his voice kind. "I have penned my sheep, so I am free to take you." He reached his hand toward Parker again.

This time, Parker did not wait so long. He was startled by how easily the boy pulled him to his feet. They stood eye to eye for a moment. Abruptly, William leaned down and, linking his fingers, said, "Give me your foot, Parker. Lean on my shoulder." The horse swung her head to look but didn't shift her weight. The Indian's shoulder felt wiry and muscular under Parker's hand. He'd been boosted onto the mare's back before he knew he was off the ground. His knees pressed against a pair of sacks slung over the animal's withers.

A moment later, William had slid up behind him and reached around for the reins.

"I can ride behind," Parker said, crossing his arms over his body and trying to keep from touching the Indian's dark skin.

"You are too weak," William said flatly.

As the Indian swung the mare's head with the reins, Parker felt the boy's knees clamp down on her sides. She bounded forward, and Parker fell against the boy's chest. He was glad for William's strong arms, too, and his eyes filled with tears again.

"O'Keeffe will shelter you," the Indian said, as the horse trotted across the desert.

"The rich lady?" Parker bounced on the horse's back. "The one that paints?"

"She has found her true home here." It sounded like something a very old man would say.

"How old are you?" Parker asked William.

"Fifteen winters, the same as you."

"How did you know how old I am?" Parker demanded.

"I have eyes."

Parker sighed. Indians never gave straight answers. They smelled strange, too. This one surely did. Sage and wood smoke and wet wool. "How soon will we get to Miss O'Keeffe's?" Parker asked.

"Soon enough, and I will leave you there," William said. Parker nodded. William was as eager to get rid of him as he was to get away from this spooky mutton puncher. Parker thought for a moment. "I suppose I should thank you for saving my life," he said.

William didn't answer. Parker gritted his teeth. That was just like an Indian, too. No manners. Parker sighed with relief when the horse pulled up beside a small white house.

"O'Keeffe's," William said. "Wait." He slid quickly off the horse and reached up his hands to help, but Parker dismounted on his own and stumbled to a bench in the shade. "Sit then," the boy said. He knocked on the heavy oak door and waited. "Painting," he said. "She will come out by and by." William offered his canteen.

As Parker raised it to his lips, the Indian was already mounting the pinto. "She has what you need," he said, shifting his weight on the horse's back. "Make sure that you deserve it." He trotted quickly back down the dry wash, the horse's hoofbeats muffled by the soft sand.

CHAPTER THREE

O'Keeffe

Parker gulped half the water left in William's canteen, and then leaned back against the stucco wall. He looked at the desert around the little house. From the Pedernal Mountain in the distance to the sharp line of shade thrown by the overhanging roof, crisp edges defined everything. This was all real: the house, the smooth adobe bench beneath his thighs, and the weight of the canteen in his hand. Parker's stomach growled. That, too, was real. So was the lingering touch of a headache. He felt as if he were awakening from a long nap. The memory of the monstrous ram he'd seen returned. Clearly that was not real. A dream? A hallucination? Parker looked at the canteen in his hand. William was no vision, he decided, slowly sipping the rest of the water.

His stomach growled again. Parker took a deep breath and stared at the dark wooden door. Perhaps this O'Keeffe had not heard William's knocks? It was time to ask, again, for food and shelter—and maybe for a job. He had done this enough in the past to know what worked. Parker waited until his mind felt clear enough, then stood, brushed the sand from his jeans, squared his collar, ran his hands through his hair, and raised his hand to knock. To his surprise, the door swung open easily on its hinges.

"Um, howdy?" Parker said softly. There was no answer. "Miss O'Keeffe?" Parker stepped into the room and stared. It was hard to believe someone actually lived there. Instead of soft chairs and rugs and ruffled curtains, the place was stripped bare. White sheets covered the sofa and chairs and the only color came from a Navajo rug on the floor. An artist's easel stood by an open window. Through the glass, the Pedernal stood solid and silent against the bright blue sky. The easel held a blank painting, with a pile of photographs stacked nearby. A clutter of pencils and brushes, rags and cups and paint tubes lay strewn around on a window ledge, and a pair of cameras seemed tossed onto a plain wooden table.

Two cameras? Clyde had been right, Parker thought. This O'Keeffe surely was rich.

The sound of a woman's cough floated from behind another door. *Ma?* The thought came too quick to block, along with the memory of Ma's coughing toward the end. Parker glanced around. Why had he just walked right in? What if the owner caught him in her house? She'd never give him a job. He stepped back toward the open door but he was too late. A tall woman in black strode through the other door and stopped.

"What are you doing here?"

Parker made his shoulders relax as he smiled broadly. He held out his hand. "I'm Parker Ray," he said. "Pleased to meet you, Miss O'Keeffe." He waited to see if it would work.

The artist stared at him. Parker made his eyes stay friendly and focused as he took in every detail. The woman pulled her hair firmly into a bun—like Ma's. But Ma was pale and gentle and scented with rosewater. This woman stood ramrod straight in a black housedress buttoned to the neck. A strange chemical odor wafted along with her.

"Well, I'll say this for you, Mr. Ray," Georgia O'Keeffe said. "You do have gall."

A straight talker, Parker thought, deciding how to answer. Not frightened, not angry.

"I've needed gall, and wits, too," he said, picking his words, "making my own way." She was nodding, so Parker went on. "I'm sore hungry, ma'am, but I never take charity. I'll work any job that needs doing around here to repay you."

"I don't have time for this," she said. When she glanced at a wristwatch, Parker was astonished at how large and strong her hands looked. "As soon as I'm done in the darkroom," she went on, "I can feed you, but there's nothing that I need."

No, Parker thought of her expensive watch. There probably isn't. The unfairness of it burned his gut as much as Clyde's whiskey had.

The artist gestured at the canteen. "You've had dealings with the Indians?"

"I guess you might say one of them saved my life. His name is William Dark Sky. If it weren't for him, I'd have died of thirst out in this dang desert."

Miss O'Keeffe stared out through the window and her face softened. "Most beautiful place I know," she said. "First time I felt its spirit, I knew this is where I belong."

Parker tried again. "I could be happy anywhere, if only it would rain," he said. In these drought years that was always a safe line to get an agreeable conversation going.

"I like it dry." She glanced at her watch again and shook her head. "Wait here," she said, and slipped through the other door.

Strange woman, Parker thought. The skin on his neck prickled at the sight of bleached bones lying in the corner by the door. Everything in this place was bones and ghosts and spirits. He moved closer. There was no magical ram's skull. He relaxed and looked at the rest of the collection. What kind of person, he wondered, would bring an old cow skull, some backbones, and a jumble of leg bones right into their house?

"How did you get in?" Miss O'Keeffe called from the back room.

"Door was open, ma'am."

"I'm not 'ma'am,'" she responded. "Just call me O'Keeffe."

"O'Keeffe." Parker tried it out very quietly. It sounded all wrong. He had never called a grown woman anything so disrespectful to her face. He knew what his ma would have said.

"Well, Parker, how would you like a sandwich?" Parker's stomach clenched so tightly he couldn't answer. She went on as if nothing had happened. "I have some lemonade and fruit, too, and I had that Clyde bring over a crock of pickles from the ranch house."

Parker walked into a dim kitchen. His mouth snapped closed against the sharp chemical stink, and his eyes watered, too. O'Keeffe didn't seem to notice as she pulled a heavy Indian blanket away from the window. Sunshine flooded in, showing trays and jars full of strong-smelling fluids on the counters. A row of photographs hung, dripping, pinned along a string like laundry. She gestured at them. "In this heat, they'll be ready by the time we finish."

"I thought you were a painter," Parker said, trying not to breathe the fumes. He wondered how she could live like this.

"I use a camera to take notes," she said. "Tone, details, fast-changing skies, possibilities." She offered him a big knife. "You cut the bread. I'll spread the butter on and the ham." When Parker looked at her in surprise, she said, "Six slices, nice and thick."

Parker took the knife, thinking how fearless she was to hand a stranger a weapon. Fearless—or foolish, just like Clyde had said. But it was a good kind of foolish. His ma had been like that. Trusting. And generous. Until she was so sick, she had helped anybody in need. Until the drought. And the dust storms.

O'Keeffe led Parker outside to the bench and sat down. "There." She took a deep breath of the fresh air. "That's better. Are two sandwiches enough for you?" she asked.

"Oh, yes, ma'am, they surely are." Parker's mouth was watering. "I haven't seen this much food at once in . . ." He stopped, unable to remember a handout this grand.

"I grew up on a farm in Wisconsin," the artist said. "I know how much it takes to feed a hard-working body. There's more bread if you want it for the road."

The road? Parker swallowed so suddenly he choked. She thumped his back until he could breathe.

"How'd a farm girl get to be a painter?" he asked, wiping his eyes. It was important to keep her talking if there was any chance of staying.

"Oh, you don't want to hear that old story," she said.

"Oh, but I do, ma'am. Please." Parker took another bite and forced himself to look attentive as he chewed instead of bolted down the food.

"I was good in art as a child," she said, "and my mother made sure I got lessons in town." Parker nodded, halfway through the first sandwich. "When they sent me away to school," the woman went on, "the sisters encouraged me. I went to art school, and then taught art here and there. I've taught them all: grade school, high school, college." She stopped and looked at Parker. "You have any talent?"

Parker shrugged and swallowed, then took another bite. Maybe he could stay with this woman, he thought. Plenty to eat here. Lady so rich she'd never miss a bit of food. It took a moment for him to notice that O'Keeffe was still waiting for an answer. "Talent? I don't reckon I have any, ma'am." He took another bite.

"Pity," the woman said. Her tone told Parker he'd failed some sort of test.

"But I never had any reason to draw or anything," he said quickly. "Always wanted to, though. Yearned to, truth be told, but nobody did any art teaching in my school. I never got my chance." He took another bite and went on, his mouth full. "Never met a real live artist before in my whole life, either." He swallowed. "It's an honor, ma'am. A true honor."

"Nonsense," O'Keeffe said. "You know nothing of me or my art. For a drifter, a full belly is the only honor that matters. Shall I fix another sandwich?"

Parker stared at her. A wide smile broke the serious look on her face. He nodded. "Yes'm, please."

While she worked inside, Parker licked his lips, savoring the sweet, salty taste of the ham and the pressure of food in his belly. He had to stay here, he decided, no matter how strange this woman and her house were. But what else could he say that would win her over? Nothing he had tried so far had made any impression.

As she strode back onto the patio, he blurted, "You remind me of my ma, Miss O'Keeffe. She died six months ago." That had to do it, he thought, but he felt his face flush with shame.

"That is hard luck," the painter said. She looked at her watch. "More lemonade, ah, Parker, before I get back to work?"

"Miss O'Keeffe, ma'am," he said quickly, "I just can't take all this without repaying you. Please let me do something for you around the place."

"It's just O'Keeffe," she corrected him. "And the only way you can repay me is to move on and let me get back to work."

Parker stopped chewing. That wasn't fair, he thought. More, it was downright mean after he had told her about Ma and all. It was like she wasn't even listening to him. And the woman had already turned her back. He heard her wide black skirts swish through the door and her boots clop on the pine floor inside. "Your canteen is on the counter here," she called. "Mind you fill it before you go."

Parker swallowed the last of the sandwich and drained the lemonade. It didn't taste as good now. He looked out at the endless desert and sighed. Two hours to sunset, he figured. Why couldn't she have offered him a place to stay the night? He grabbed his plate and cup and headed indoors.

"Don't you even think to open this door," the painter called from the kitchen. "The room has to stay dark for the photographs."

Not even a good-bye? Turned out into the desert night after I near died, Parker thought. She forgot the packet of food to go, too, though she'd as good as promised it. He glared around the room and set his plate and cup on the table beside her brushes. It wouldn't have hurt her to help me, he thought. She had so much. He couldn't guess how much all those fancy tubes of paint cost, or the mug of brushes. He stared at the cameras. They were fancy ones. Either one of them probably cost almost five whole dollars, he thought. He'd have to work a full week at a good job to earn that much. It might even be enough to buy a room for a night at the Ghost Ranch and some grub for the trip. Wherever the trip was going.

He picked up one of the cameras, careful not to let it clatter against anything on the table. It was surprisingly light. Parker looked around. A hundred paintbrushes, a house all to herself, and two whole cameras. Clyde was right. She was weird and she was rich—and she was too mean to share. Miss O'Keeffe, he decided, was going to give him a him a bed for a night, one way or another.

Parker tucked her camera under his arm and quietly stole out the door.

CHAPTER FOUR

Click!

"What you got there, boy?"

Parker froze. Before he could toss the camera into a nearby sage-brush, a slender figure stepped out from behind a crumbling roadside bluff. The man's hand rested on a holster at his hip and a sheriff's star hung from his vest, but his face looked friendly. Simple, Parker thought. This one should be easy to outthink.

He pulled himself up. Parker knew how officers handled drifters, and he had no wish to be manhandled—or worse—today. "Good afternoon, sir," he said. "Mind if I take your picture?" He held the camera up between his face and the sheriff's and kept talking. "I'm new at the Ghost Ranch, yonder. Been taking pictures of the colored cliffs hereabouts."

"I bet," the man said, but his voice had lost its edge.

"Oh, yes, sir." Parker pressed his advantage. "The old folks will pay a pretty penny for these little scenes." He fiddled with the lens and pressed a button that made a satisfying *click*. He wound the crank to move new film into place like the traveling photographer had done at home between shots of his family. Parker searched his mind for words the photographer had said when he came to the farm. "Step back a bit now, sir. Tilt your head, just a mite, and hold it."

"Who are you trying to fool?" The man's voice was skeptical, but through the viewfinder, Parker saw that his head was slightly tilted.

"Nice," Parker said, trying to remember some of Georgia O'Keeffe's artist words, too. "I'm just looking for tone, details, and fast-changing skies, here," he muttered. Through the viewfinder, he saw an eagle soar up into the clouds behind the sheriff's hat. He tilted the camera to follow the bird's flight and snapped the shutter.

"You staying out there with the Packs? Arthur and Phoebe Pack?" the lawman asked, craning his head to peer into the sky.

"Nope." Parker stooped and took a picture of the man's hat, the eagle, and the Pedernal Mountain in the distance. "Nice shot," he breathed.

"Who'd you say you were staying with at the ranch?" The man had turned back. Parker busied himself with the camera a minute before answering.

"I just came down to see Clyde. That was just fine with, ah, Phoebe and Arthur. But then, being as we are both creative types, Miss O'Keeffe invited me to stay on with her."

"Now I know you are lying, boy. That lady doesn't want anybody anywhere near her. Closest thing to a hermit I ever saw," the lawman said. "Now hand me that camera."

"It's not mine to give you, sir. It is Miss O'Keeffe's. She loaned it to me so I could try out a really fine model instead of my dusty old-fashioned box. With that one, I had to set up a tripod and throw a black cloth over my head and—"

"We'll see about that," the lawman said. He drew his gun and waved it toward the road. "If you'll just come with me, we'll go have a bit of a chat with the lady herself."

"Sheriff Young? I don't have time for this," O'Keeffe said as she stood in the door.

"This yours?" he asked her.

Parker felt her blue eyes rake over him. "*This* is a young man, a drifter, named Parker Ray," she said. "Bright, homeless orphan from Texas, polite and probably getting hungry again." Parker stared at her in surprise.

"That's not what I meant. Is this your *camera*?" Sheriff Young held it out to her.

O'Keeffe's stern mouth tightened even more as she took it from him. She looked the camera over. "It is still working. Near a full roll of film gone, though. You a photo artist?" she asked Parker sharply.

Sheriff Young shook his head. "He is an artist, all right. A con artist. I need to take him back to Espanola to the lockup until you decide if you want to press charges. And we need to telegraph back down Texas way to learn if this Parker has pulled anything worse."

"No need to do that, sir," Parker said quickly. "No need at all."

"You sure are a smooth talker, son," Sheriff Young said, turning the car around in the road. "You had me going there. How old are you?"

"Twenty, sir."

"Now, don't you go spinning me more lies. My oldest son is almost your age. Shall we call you fifteen?"

"Yes, sir," Parker mumbled.

"You been walking the road a good long while to wear out your boots like that. And you've grown two inches since those pants were new. No family left?" Parker stayed silent until the lawman grunted and went on. "You come from down Texas way, by your accent. Most of the Texas farms, like the rest of the Dust Bowl, purely blew away in the last few years. Families scattered with the dust. From the cracks in your lips you been mighty dried out lately. You thirsty again?" He threw a canteen across the seat.

Parker sat still, amazed. How could this man see so much in such a short time? The sheriff glanced back and went on. "Crumbs on your shirt. Did O'Keeffe give you enough to eat?" Parker didn't answer. "We better get you fattened up some or those pants will fall right off your legs."

"You have a big family?" Parker had to ask.

"Me and the missus got us four boys."

Parker nodded. He had nearly drained the sheriff's canteen by the time they stopped in a dusty little town. He followed wearily into a small adobe office. "There's the cell," the lawman said, pointing through a back door. "Your new home. You get lonely, you just call, you hear? Bed in there and a blanket. Seems a long, safe sleep might be what you need, 'less you want another drink first."

There was an Indian blanket and a pillow, too. And a small high window and a barred door. Sheltered by thick adobe walls, the air was stale but cool and shadowy. Parker stretched out on the bed, telling himself he would listen for the front door. When Parker rested his eyes, he only meant to close them for a moment.

"Where *is* he?" Georgia O'Keeffe's imperious voice filled the little building. Parker awoke. After three days, he'd given up hope that she would forgive him. Three days—he smiled—of sleep and water, and all the food he could eat. "Show him to me!" Sharp footsteps clicked across the tiles, then her tall, thin form passed the desk and turned to fill the barred doorway. "Unlock this," she said. The deputy bent and fumbled with the keys. "Hurry!" the artist insisted.

"I am dropping charges," she announced. "Follow me, Parker." She swept out the door.

Parker followed her, blinking in the harsh New Mexico sunlight. "But the camera?" he asked.

"You will work off your crime at my place," she said. "It will take you a month."

Parker looked at her. There was no warmth in her face. "What are you waiting for? Get into my car."

Parker stared at the Model A. He could not suppress a grin. "Yes, ma'am, Miss O'Keeffe."

"It's just 'O'Keeffe'," she snapped.

CHAPTER FIVE

Carrot Juice

"Whoa," Parker said as they careened around the first turn heading back to Ghost Ranch.

"I want to be home while there is still light to work."

Parker looked at the sun, low in the sky, and shook his head. It had taken almost two hours to drive there in the sheriff's car, he thought. He braced himself as O'Keeffe slammed on the brakes to avoid hitting a cow and her calf. The animals looked at them dully, and then moved on. She gunned the engine.

"Been driving long?" Parker asked, once he'd caught his breath.

"Couple of years," she answered. "This is my first car."

"Nice. A Model A, right?" Parker said. Then he looked into the back. "What in tarnation happened to it?" He had to ask. Model As had wide, comfortable seating, plenty of leg room, and big windows, but the entire backseat of this one had been torn out. Tidy boxes and tubes crowded the empty space. A big water jug sat in the middle of the floor, and huge pads of paper were wedged against one window.

"It is mine," O'Keeffe said. "This is how I want it."

"Oh." She left no opening for Parker to ask why. He struggled to find something else to say. "My pa's Model A was the cat's pajamas. Me and Ma used to both sit up front in the rainstorms, singing loud as the thunder itself." He grinned to himself, remembering how it felt.

"I always thought that singing was the perfect means of expression." She seemed to be talking to herself.

"When we felt poor," Parker told her, "we'd sing, 'Brother, Can You Spare a Dime?' But the happy songs are better. Like 'Camptown Races'." He launched into a spirited chorus of "do dah, do dah," but trailed off when he realized that she wasn't joining in.

"I can't carry a tune," she said. "Since I don't sing, I paint."

"Oh," Parker said. He tried to remember a time when his ma wasn't singing. Hymns, nursery songs, or even nonsense songs she made up. Pa kept saying he'd get her a piano, until the drought hit hard. Parker looked through the windshield at the sky. A thunderhead glowered over the mountains, lightning flickering in its dark base. "Think that cloud will bring rain?" he asked hopefully. O'Keeffe didn't answer. Parker winced. She had said she liked it dry.

"Sure is purty country," he tried again.

"Yup," she said. "I can't get enough of just looking at it." When Parker took a breath to speak again, she repeated firmly, "I said *just looking* at it."

They "just looked" in silence for the next hour as the scenery rolled—and bounced—by. Once or twice, O'Keeffe stopped the car at the crest of a hill overlooking the dry Chama River or down in a gully filled with carved red rocks. She would take a deep, deep breath—and just look. Once she mentioned that the light was perfect, "at an angle to make the shadows deep and rich." So Parker "just looked" at that. Later she told him to notice how the sunset reflected off one cliff face onto another.

"You sure do talk like a schoolteacher."

"I am a painter now," she said firmly, and went on looking. Parker glanced at her face. For all the fierceness in her tone, her face softened when she looked at the desert. There was no softness when she looked at him. What on earth did she want with him, he wondered. She already had her camera back.

The Model A swerved suddenly on a hill. Parker thought first of Clyde's tortoises, but the tilt of the car told him something was wrong. He stiffened as they headed toward the ditch. Parker grabbed the handle to steady himself but O'Keeffe slowly pulled the automobile to the edge of the dirt road. As she switched off the gasoline valve, an unmistakable hissing sound floated through Parker's open window. "Flat tire?" he asked, bracing himself for the storms of tears that had always followed breakdowns in his family car.

"Good thing I carry two spares," O'Keeffe said calmly. She stepped out and found rocks to use as chocks, jamming them under the tires. "Jack is in the trunk," she said, "and the rest of the tools." Parker stared at her. The trousers covering her long legs suddenly looked very practical. No one, he thought, could do this in a housedress.

"Well?" She stood grinning at him, holding the spare wheel, its steel spokes glistening in the late-afternoon light. She is enjoying this! Parker thought. He scrambled to get the jack and, working together, they had the tire switched before the sun hit the horizon.

She carefully clipped the ruined wheel to the door, jumped back in, and told him to move the chocks. Then they were off. In minutes, they turned from the dirt road at the sign of a cow's skull. A bell began ringing. "Think you can eat again?" she asked. "That early bell means chow time for the hands." She pulled the auto along a field of soft green and parked it under a big old cottonwood.

"Follow me," she said, and strode off toward another little adobe building with a beehive-shaped oven out in the yard. Plank tables were set about in the shade. A handful of men sat at the tables, shoveling beans onto slabs of bread, picking their teeth, or slurping from coffee mugs even bigger than those at the jail. They all looked up briefly, stared at Parker, elbowed one another, and went back to eating. Parker looked around for Clyde. He didn't seem to be there.

"The guests will eat in another hour," O'Keeffe told him as they sat down at empty places. "Mostly I just eat with the ranch hands. They leave me alone to think."

A girl with bright eyes and long dangling earrings set plates before them and mugs of water. "I'll have carrot juice, Merita," O'Keeffe said. "So will my boy."

Parker stiffened. He was nobody's "boy." And he'd never heard of carrot juice.

"Sí." The waitress looked at Parker and smiled, then ducked her head and scurried off toward the building. She came back with a small pitcher full of liquid, thick as cane syrup and a vile orange color. Her long dark hair brushed Parker's hand as she poured for him.

"They work the help hard here," O'Keeffe said, "and pay them

little. That's why she's angling like that for tips." Parker's hand was
tingling from the older girl's touch.

"Tips?" he repeated, his voice breaking as it hadn't done in years.

"Drink up," O'Keeffe said, as Merita strolled away. "Good for
your eyes." Parker stared at the cup. "You're not my mother," he
wanted to say, but the ranch hands were watching. He wiped the
plate clean and drank down the water, but did not touch the strange
juice. "Your loss," O'Keeffe said. She swung her legs over the bench.
"I'm heading out for my evening rounds," she said. "I have to say
'good-night' to my desert. I'm sure Merita will be happy to bring you
pie if you want." She waved to the waitress across the tables. Parker
sank in his chair as she went on. "We're staying in the garden casita,
Parker. Anyone can tell you where that is. Be nice if you light a
kerosene lantern there before the generator is turned off for the night.
And sweep the courtyard."

Before he could argue, she strode away toward the mesa behind
the cookhouse.

"Sweep?" he muttered. "She wants her boy to sweep for her?"

"Sí, señor?" Merita stood at his elbow in a cloud of spicy perfume
and reached across him for their plates.

"Pie" was all he could manage to say. Merita nodded and laughed.
Then she turned and winked to a table of ranch hands lounging over
their coffee.

Parker and his pie were nearly the last customers left as the tables
were reset for the official guests' dinners. Shiny white tablecloths
had been laid on the empty tables, and Merita was reaching on tiptoe
to light candles in tall candleholders. Parker noticed the way the

light reflecting upward from the cloths lit the creamy undersides of her arms. She seemed to be too busy to return his glance. He looked up into the trees overhead in frustration, and saw reflected light there, too. It was like the light in the mountains that O'Keeffe had shown him. He looked away. He didn't want to think of O'Keeffe now. Or here.

When Merita bustled by for his plates, Parker asked directions to the garden casita. "The last house down the road," she said. "You have a lantern?" Parker shook his head no and stood watching as she hurried over to clear plates from the last two men sitting at the tables. Parker hitched up his jeans and ambled off in the direction Merita had pointed.

The road lay in deep shadow, cast by a ridge that ringed the Ghost Ranch to the west. The windows of three or four little houses glowed brightly from under the trees. Houses for the guests, Parker realized. The Eastern dudes. Suddenly the electricity died. As his eyes adjusted, Parker saw a softer yellow glow at the windows. The sound of the ranch had changed, too. Without the generator running, it was quieter. Now Parker heard wind in the dry field, insects calling in the treetops, and crickets singing, too. Somewhere an owl hooted. A horse was clop-clopping slowly up the road behind him.

"Well, if it ain't Dust Boy again!" Clyde's voice cut through the soft night air. Parker swung around. "I hear tell you paid Sheriff Young a visit," Clyde said. "Word is, O'Keeffe lost a camera and found herself a boy. You know anything about that all?"

Parker stared up into the darkness. Instead of Clyde's voice, he heard a girl speak softly with a thick Spanish accent. "You know this one, *mi amor*?" she said.

"That's just the yahoo I saved in the desert," Clyde answered. "I told you. He's a no-account."

As they came closer, Merita peeked out from behind Clyde's large form on the horse.

"What is his name?" she asked.

"My name is Parker, señorita, Parker Ray."

"Like Quanna Parker, the war chief of the Comanches?" she asked. Parker found himself grinning, astonished that anyone outside Texas would know about the famous Parker.

"Don't matter what you call him," Clyde interrupted brusquely. "Parker's leaving soon. Maybe tomorrow." There was menace in his tone. As his eyes adjusted, Parker could see the warning in Clyde's face, too.

"Sorry, Clyde. I have to hang around the ranch a month," Parker said. "Sheriff's orders. You're stuck with me." He addressed Merita, whose enormous eyes showed now, dark and startled, like a deer's. "May I look for you, señorita . . .?"

"You have your own girl," Clyde hissed. "If you can call her that. You jus' stay away from mine." Parker saw him jerk the horse's reins and kick at his sides. The animal tucked his hindquarters and spun, then cantered off down the road.

"*Buenas noches,* señorita," Parker called after them. It was all the Spanish he knew. In a month, he thought, he could probably learn more.

A cough sounded behind him, and Parker jumped. "Good evening, young sir," a man said. He carried a glowing lantern in one hand. An elegantly dressed woman clung to his other arm, pearls and gemstones sparkling around her neck. Parker thought his own clothes looked like rags.

"Good evening, ma'am," he said, tipping an imaginary hat, "and sir. Mighty fine night for a walk." He stepped aside to let them pass. Other lanterns were heading toward the cookhouse. A half-dozen greetings later, Parker was alone again. A piano began playing softly near the supper tables, and the gentle laughter of party guests floated over the dude ranch. There was no more Clyde in the dark and no sound of hooves on the sandy road.

Parker stumbled on down the lane, squinting into the darkness. Ahead of him, the golden glow of a lantern flared. He headed for it. "That you, Parker?" O'Keeffe's voice called out. He passed the bench he remembered, and then he entered the little house, the last one on the road. Beyond it, he knew, was nothing but desert; desert, dry washes, and sidewinders like Clyde.

"Nice job of sweeping," said O'Keeffe, glancing at the mess that still littered the patio. "I'm sleeping on the roof tonight. You?"

"Why?" Parker asked.

"Because I am tired."

"I mean why would you sleep outside, on the roof?"

"Why don't you try it and see?" O'Keeffe tossed him an Indian blanket and headed out the door. Parker shrugged to no one and followed. It was a challenge to climb the long ladder with the heavy blanket, but O'Keeffe hadn't paused on the way—and she was carrying the lantern, too.

"Just look at the stars," she said, turning out the lantern. Suddenly the skies were alight with thousands of sparkling dots. Even when he'd had to sleep outside on the road, Parker had never really looked—"just looked"—before. He spread the blanket and wrapped himself in its thick wool against the cool desert air.

Thousands of stars put the ridges and spires of rock that ringed the Ghost Ranch into glowing silhouette. The Milky Way was a smeary path bright enough to walk across. Parker wanted to ask O'Keeffe if she knew which was the North Star and where the Big Dipper hung, but the longer he looked, the more stars he saw. They had colors, too: faint pink and blue, ruddy and gold. Some fell. Others twinkled and spun. Finally, their names didn't matter, and Parker lay pressed to the adobe roof by the weight of thousands of stars.

CHAPTER SIX

Bones

Parker had no idea what first awakened him, but in the early light, he saw O'Keeffe standing at the far edge of the roof, silent. He wondered if she was going to jump. Then he wondered what she was peering at, out over the edge. He propped himself up on one elbow and looked.

It was just the butte, deep brown and sandblasted smooth by desert winds and carved deeply by sudden rains. He shrugged and yawned and laid down again, pulling the blanket over himself against the night's deep chill.

When he opened his eyes again, she was still there, a statue against the brightening sky. As far as he could reckon, she hadn't moved one bit. He pushed up on his elbow. The air leaking in under the blanket was already warm. This day would be a scorcher, he told himself. The clouds were coloring up now, taking on a faded pink. He remembered that color from one of his mother's old housedresses, washed so many times it was almost a rag by the end.

He shook the memory free and looked at O'Keeffe. She was

already dressed, trousers and shirt as black as the bandanna that wrapped her tightly bunned hair. A black shawl wound around her shoulders held out the morning breeze. Parker watched as she jerked her hand up to stuff a few loose strands of hair back under control. He smiled and looked back up at the housedress pink sky.

But now the clouds were shreds of flaming rose, burning brighter than campfire embers. His mother would never wear such a color. Parker sat up. The adobe edges of the house had turned pink. O'Keeffe's loose hairs, too, reflected the dawn sky. Now the butte beyond had come alive. The rocks looked almost bloodred, their color trickling down to black in the twisted gullies. Then the sun rose. In an instant, the top of the mesa was creamy tan again, the sun-bleached color of normal rock.

Parker let out his breath.

O'Keeffe turned at the sound, her face pink and soft. She nodded curtly at him and went back to watching the rocks.

Parker stood and pulled on his boots. He hurried down the ladder and quickly found a bush behind a low wall. As he stood watering the plant, he couldn't keep his eyes off the butte. Where had all its color gone? He'd seen blood and black and cream there. He tried to remember the burning clouds over all, but now the sky held only wisps of white against drought blue. The butte had gone back to faint tints of its dawn colors.

O'Keeffe scuttled down the ladder and whisked into the house. Parker quickly buttoned up and wandered in after her, his stomach telling him it was time for breakfast. Hush, he told it. He was getting spoiled by three meals a day. He rubbed his hand over his belly. It was flat for a change instead of a hollow cave.

Don't get used to this, he reminded himself. You have to get to California. That's where most of the drifters said there were jobs. That's what Pa had said before he left.

"Parker?" came the sharp voice.

"Yes, ma'am?" He ambled into the kitchen.

"That's just O'Keeffe," she snapped. Then she added, "Juice." She strode on toward the painting room. Parker picked up a glass of carrot-colored liquid, shrugged, and tasted it. He was licking the sweet rich taste off his lips as he came to see what O'Keeffe was doing. The artist leaned over a box holding hundreds of cards. Her fingers flicked through the files, pulling out slips here and there and, just as quickly, shoving them back into place.

"What are you looking for?" Parker asked.

She didn't answer, so he moved closer. Each of the slips was painted a different color, he saw. O'Keeffe was sorting through the browns, pulling darker and redder shades. She seemed to settle on two or three, then flipped them over to read their backs. Parker only caught a flash of what looked like recipes before she slapped the cards onto the windowsill and dug back into the box. Now she selected creams and dark purples. When she had about a dozen paint chips, O'Keeffe placed them carefully on the counter and stood staring at them in silence: bloods, blacks, and creams.

It was the butte, Parker realized. She'd matched its colors exactly. Or rather, the sunrise colors that were gone forever.

He wandered back into the kitchen, wondering what she was

going to do with the paint swatches. He didn't bother to ask. She was clearly not in the mood to answer questions. Parker poured himself another glass of juice from a tin pitcher he found in an electric refrigerator. As he stood there, the lights suddenly came on. The refrigerator hummed. In the distance, he could hear the generator running again, and a bell rang. Parker wondered if that meant breakfast time.

O'Keeffe stalked through. "Want to walk with me?" she asked. Parker looked at her in surprise. "Well then, while I roam this morning, you can do the chores you didn't quite get to last night," she said. "Keep an eye out for scorpions, you hear?"

Parker was dozing in the courtyard when the front gate squeaked on its hinges. He leaped up at the sound of Merita's voice. *"Buenos dias,"* she said, padding across the patio on slender bare feet.

"Buenos dias, señorita," Parker said quickly. He stared at her. If anything, the swirls of braids piled high on her head made her neck look longer. So did an intricate cross hanging low—very low—against her skin on a gold chain. She looked older. Too old for you, he cautioned himself. He brushed the dust off his Levis.

"You have missed breakfast," she said, smiling. "I'm sure I could find something for you. . . ."

Parker had trouble breathing.

Suddenly O'Keeffe swept in through the gate and nodded to Merita. "I see, Parker, that you still have not picked up." She stared at the ground. Suddenly Parker was aware of snowdrifts of cottonwood seeds and dead leaves still lying in the corners of the yard.

"I was working on up to it," he said. The housemaid's earrings tinkled as she shook her head at him. Parker smiled back and reached for the rake he had leaned against the casita.

"Don't touch that," O'Keeffe said. He froze. Had she seen a scorpion? A tarantula? A rattler? Adrenaline flooded his body. He watched tensely as she made a slow semicircle, staring at the debris pile by the bench. She stopped and studied the leaves, then reached toward them, silently. Parker eased his hand to the rake and picked it up, holding it ready.

But O'Keeffe was just picking up two dead leaves. She cradled them in her hands, twisting them this way and that, then turned and walked into the house. Parker's eyes met the girl's, and they both shrugged their shoulders and grinned.

"Parker, after breakfast we will go out in the car," O'Keeffe announced. "I want you where I can keep an eye on you." Parker sighed. Three good meals a day and a safe, if strange, house—but he was still the artist's prisoner. For a month. Why? He thought back to the jail. Even there nobody was as crazy as her. Parker glanced at Merita again. Or, he thought, as pretty as Clyde's girl. He followed O'Keeffe in to see her set the leaves down carefully beside the paint chips and stare at them. Parker stared, too. Their colors matched exactly.

Without turning, O'Keeffe asked, "Merita? Do you know where the skulls went that I collected last summer?"

"Sí, señora," the girl said, and made the sign of the cross. She went on to describe where she and Clyde had dumped the skulls. Parker wasn't listening. Merita had called her "señora." O'Keeffe was *married*? Parker couldn't imagine why anyone would want this strange woman for a wife. And where was he? Then suddenly he was listening closely again.

"The ram's skull, Merita. Is it with the others?"

Parker pictured the ram's skull, dead on the sand. Alive over him. Towering above him, silken wool flowing like a waterfall, horns like swords. He reached a hand to the counter to steady himself.

"Sí, it is there, with the others."

"Parker, we'll grab us a breakfast and head out. Get the camera for me, will you?" With one last delicate touch to the leaves, O'Keeffe was ready to go.

"What do you want with skulls?" Parker broke the silence as the Model A bumped along down the road.

He had almost decided she was ignoring him again when O'Keeffe finally answered. "To me," she said, "they are as beautiful as anything I know."

"Dead *bones*?" Parker asked.

"They seem more living sometimes than the animals that are walking around." O'Keeffe paused to downshift and turn off onto a smaller road, even more rutted than the first. "The desert is so vast and empty and untouchable, Parker. It knows no kindness, for all of its beauty. It makes the bones seem so alive by contrast."

Parker knew all about them seeming alive. "What is so special about this ram's skull?" he made himself ask.

"I am haunted by it," she said. The hairs rose on Parker's forearms. "I completed a painting of it last summer, but I haven't quite caught its spirit yet." She pulled off onto an even smaller track. "The reviews were excellent, but the skull just keeps coming back to me." Parker knew what she meant. A ram's skull had haunt- ed his dreams—and his daydreams, too—since that strange day in the desert.

"You have to paint it again?" Parker asked, but O'Keeffe had stopped the car, hauled up on the emergency brake, and bounced out the door. She stood, hands on her hips, staring up at a cliff of color- ful rocks. Parker glanced at it, and his stomach turned. He looked around quickly. There were the wash and the dry, rusted windmill. There, the juniper bush, and by it, the white-and-red boulders.

"This will do," she said. "I'm going to sketch awhile, then take a break and search for the ram's skull."

"You don't have to," Parker said quietly. "I know just where it is. I'll get it for you."

Parker climbed the rise alone. It had seemed much steeper when he had staggered the distance, looking for water. He wasn't lurching now, but his steps slowed as he neared the boulders. There he had tripped. There he had crawled. There he had looked up. His eyes traced a path where cactus and scrub grass lay smashed and burned, as if something as powerful as lightning had struck the ground.

And there was the skull. The tips of its horns were split and broken. Parker took a shaky breath and scolded himself. "Old bones," he said aloud. "Just old, dry bones," though he could not come to look into the skull's empty eye sockets. Parker made himself reach down and pick up the skull—and nearly dropped it. The horns were warm as living skin in his hands. From the sun, he told himself as he carried the skull back toward the Model A.

"You found it!" O'Keeffe said. She climbed out of the backseat of the car and ran toward him. "Oh, so beautiful," she said. "So *alive*." Parker stared as she wrapped her arms around the skull and patted it like a living animal. Her fingers, long and tan, felt over the smooth white spaces and dipped into the eyeholes. "So beautiful," she breathed again.

Her hands caressed the twisting horns, following the turns to their tips. At the splintered end, she stopped and crooned, "Oooh." Parker glanced at her face. It was soft, her eyes almost closed. He thought suddenly of his mother, gently soothing his forehead from a fever. He cleared his throat.

O'Keeffe's eyes focused on him, and then she looked down. "Is it time yet for water?"

CHAPTER SEVEN

Shade

"Enough," O'Keeffe said, corking the big water jug. She straightened her wide-brimmed black hat and stared at the rock cliff. Parker squinted in the harsh sunlight, trying to see what could be so interesting about the hill. It was more colorful than most of the badlands he'd wandered through, but it was just dry old rocks. It echoed, too, he remembered.

He leaned against the hood of the car and watched as her body settled into a silence as deep as the clefts in the giant rock face.

"What do you want me to do?" he wanted to ask. He decided to wait until she spoke to him first, no matter how long it took. Parker looked back over the low plain of desert scrub and took a deep breath. Tufts of sagebrush and juniper dotted the plain. Here and there, a cholla cactus stood knee high, bristling with spines. Nothing moved.

Suddenly O'Keeffe bustled back to the car. She reached into the back and pulled out her camera. She walked to the spot where she'd stood and stared into the viewfinder, and took two pictures of the

cliff. Then she took off to the east, her long strides covering a sur-
prising distance.

O'Keeffe didn't turn. She seemed to have forgotten Parker was
there. Every few paces, she stopped and stood, motionless, looking at
the cliff. Every time she stopped she looked smaller, but in the clear
desert air, she didn't look much farther away. Once or twice she took
pictures. When she disappeared around the edge of the bluff, Parker
pushed his body off the car and jogged after her.

When he saw her, she wasn't moving again. Parker finally recognized what she was doing. This was the "just looking" she had
spoken of on the roof, concentrating harder than a cat by a mouse
hole. He looked at the cliff. What was she trying to catch? She
didn't flinch at the sound of his boots approaching on the dry,
sandy soil or glance up as a bluebird swooped past. She didn't
speak, either, so Parker stayed silent. He trailed after her while
she looked at the cliff from three other spots and took another set
of photos.

"Fetch the car." She broke her silence. "And meet me by that big
juniper." Parker blinked. She was trusting him to drive her car now?
He tried to remember whether he'd ever told her he knew how to
drive. "Hurry," she scolded, "before the light changes."

"Yes, ma'am." Parker set off at a run. He was panting as he sat
on the front seat, trying to remember starting the old car at home,
his pa sitting alongside, coaching. Now a ram's skull sat beside
Parker. "Dry old bones," he reminded himself. "Nothing more."
He depressed the clutch, pushed the starter button, and gave the
Model A some gas. The sputter of the engine echoed off the cliff, so

he let up on the gas. The engine died, though the echo continued. Parker felt his face flush. The next time he tried, the automobile coughed and shuddered and died again, but not until he had put it into gear. He glanced at O'Keeffe. In the strange clear air, he could see she was grinning at him. On the third try, he got the car moving. It bounced and bumped along the rough ground, slung so high it cleared rocks more than a foot tall. Finally, Parker turned it off and hauled smartly on the emergency brake.

She was still grinning, so Parker got out and bowed with a flourish. "Your car, ma'am," he said.

"O'Keeffe," she corrected absently, pushing past him to get into the back of the automobile. She propped a square of white canvas up where the seat should have been. Then she looked from the white fabric to the cliff and back, slowly and silently. At last she broke into motion again, opening and closing neatly labeled boxes. From some she took crumpled tubes. Others she simply closed again and returned to the pile. Now she took brushes from a bucket on the floor and pulled a small pane of glass from a carton. Parker moved closer to see.

"Go find something to do," she said without looking up. "Take the camera. There's a few shots left on it."

Parker backed away.

"The camera," she reminded him.

Parker shook his head. The camera. What was she thinking? But he picked it up from the front seat and headed off to the old windmill. He lay down in its dust-dry trough and took a picture straight up through the rusty old blades at the clouds high above. Sitting up, he could see that she was painting. Parker wanted to go and watch, but her message had been clear.

He looked back at her from the boulders until a sharp chittering sound caught his attention. Parker tracked it down to a crevice between two boulders, where a cranky bat was trying to sleep out the day. He took a picture of the angry animal and went on. He slid down a wind-scoured slope and took a picture of some swallow nests.

Parker licked his lips. His stomach was telling him lunchtime had passed, and the heat was making him sleepy. He headed back to the Model A. O'Keeffe didn't want him to watch her paint, but with the sun high in the sky and the desert baking around them, she had to let him have some water.

There was no one in the car when he got there, though the front door stood open. Parker looked in and stared at the canvas. Broad bands of yellow and white and red covered it from side to side. There was no blue sky. There were no scrubby plants, either. Parker stood up and looked at the cliff.

The rock layers were there in real life, in almost the colors she'd painted. How, he wondered, could she leave out the blue sky? And why bother to spend all that time looking just to paint bands? Parker remembered his favorite painting. It hung in his Sunday School room and showed Noah's Ark wedged on the very top of a mountain. That picture looked so real, he had always felt he could walk right into it, climb the mountain, and knock on old Noah's door. That was really good art. He felt like laughing aloud. This Georgia O'Keeffe was a pretty sorry painter!

He wondered where she'd gone. A raven's harsh cry was the only sound he heard above the steady hot wind. There was no lunch. Just the car. Parker looked at it and wondered if he could drive it all the way to California. In all his life, he would never be able to buy a vehicle like this. He looked around quickly. O'Keeffe was gone.

He pointed the camera into the car and looked through the viewfinder. The ram's skull stared back at him. Parker almost dropped the camera. Then he looked at the front seat. The skull was lying there where he'd tossed it. Looking through the camera again, Parker was amazed to see how important the skull looked when it filled the picture, how ancient, lying in the sunshine on black leather. He clicked the shutter.

Parker swung the camera toward the backseat. Now the viewfinder focused on the tidy boxes of paint tubes, each with its hand-printed label. They made Parker think of O'Keeffe standing tall, dressed in neatly pressed black in the middle of the desert. She might not be much of a painter, but she sure was a character. He could stick it out with her for a month.

He yawned and reached for the water jug. After glancing at the cups, he held the jug right to his lips and tilted it to the sky. Suddenly something grabbed his ankle. "What?" he yelled, and tried to jump back. But his ankle was held tight and he twisted, still shouting. The water splashed down his shirt and he fell, landing on his butt in the soft sand, the jug in his lap.

Parker stared at his leg. There was nothing holding it—but there *had* been. He rolled over onto his knees and crawled closer to the car, peeking into the deep shadow beneath.

"Boo!" O'Keeffe's voice rang out, followed by a wicked cackle.

"What in tarnation!"

"Go find your own shade for a siesta, partner. This space is taken."

Parker grinned. He retreated to the deep shadows under the juniper bush and sat down, gently. His backside hurt, but the breeze was cooler out of the sunshine. The water drying on his shirt felt like a patch of the morning's chill. Parker yawned. He laid on his back, closed his eyes, and smiled, thinking about O'Keeffe's trick.

The low rumble of thunder awoke him. Parker sat up. Brisk, puffy winds had the juniper branches whipping back and forth, and a cloud covered the sun. Parker looked to the mountain ridges. The little white puffs over the peaks had grown and darkened while he dozed. The air was still hot, but it seemed alive, rushing about before the storm.

Parker squinted at the road, where dust was kicking up in the wind. As he watched, dust swirled upward like a phantom tornado. First there was just a thin line of shimmering air, then a twisting strand of blowing sand, then a full writhing dust devil. It danced left and right, growing in power until it was uprooting little grass tufts, tossing them aside. Parker pulled his bandanna up over his nose and mouth.

The dust devil turned and skittered toward the Model A, weakening as it came. "Miss O'Keeffe!" Parker shouted. "Miss O'Keeffe! Dust devil!" he called. "Get something over your face!"

The artist rolled out from under the car, took one look at the oncoming danger, and plunged into the backseat. Then he, too, was running. She had rolled up the back window by the time he had yanked open the front door and slid onto the seat. Parker slammed the door against the dust. He fought to turn the window handles up as fast as his arm could move.

The dust devil rocked the car when it hit; then it blew on. Parker and O'Keeffe stared through the window as it bounced off the cliff and died. The sand it had held aloft sifted downward, hissing against the Model A's hood.

"Close call," she said. She examined the canvas carefully, picking a few sand grains from the wet paint with a rag. "This could have been bad."

Parker looked out the window. "Look, O'Keeffe, everything's going to be fine," he said, his spirits rising. "Rain's coming for sure." Lightning bolts shot down to the mountaintops, and the shadow of rain fell straight down beneath the thundercloud. "I haven't seen rain since . . ." He struggled to remember.

"Not going to happen today," she said. "Get out. I'm driving." She got behind the wheel, and they rolled down the windows again as they headed home. Along the road, Parker watched gray curtains of rain falling thousands of feet from the cloud high overhead. He watched the raindrops dry up, too, long before they hit. For hundreds of feet above their heads, the air was dust dry. The only part of the storm that reached the ground was rumbling thunder and white-hot lightning.

Though the mountains were distant, Parker could see fires

burning where lightning had struck along the ridges. There was no rain to put the fires out. "We need a real rain." He sighed.

"If the wind holds, we'll be able to smell the fires up on the roof tonight," O'Keeffe said. "Tomorrow we will come out and paint some more."

CHAPTER EIGHT

Fans

Parker stole a glance at the painting in its backseat space. For two days now, O'Keeffe had worked darker shading into the bands of color, and brushstroke by brushstroke, the cliffs had taken form. They would never support Noah's Ark. They looked more like ice cream, all soft and melting together, than like real mountains. For some reason, she seemed happy with it. Parker wondered what a real artist would do with the rugged scene around them. He turned away quickly as she got in behind the wheel.

"This is the last day on this painting," she said. "Were those new photographs dry enough to bring along?" Parker nodded. He patted a folder lying on the seat between them. After dinner early in the week, O'Keeffe had hurried back to the casita to push the dead leaves around yet again on the windowsill. She moved them this way and that and finally stood staring at them so long that Parker thought she might have dozed off standing there. He had also thought he was done for the night.

She'd called him to the kitchen and showed him how to develop film. That first night, the film had to be soaked in trays of chemicals that smelled so bitter Parker could still taste them on his tongue. In the baths, in darkness, the film had produced negatives, but wet ones. Parker had rearranged O'Keeffe's clotheslines over the kitchen sink where negatives hung to dry. The strings were knotted neatly now, taut and tidy. Other than that, he had followed her directions precisely, though he was yawning by the time he emptied the last tray of chemicals back into its glass bottle, corked it tight, and wiped the counter dry.

The next night after dinner, she had showed him how to make prints from the negatives. He used more chemicals that tasted like metal in the air, more trays, more darkness, and then, magically, photographs appeared on the special paper she kept under the sink. The photos were beauties, he thought as he laid them to dry on screens, but it had been a shock to see the brightly colored cliffs in black-and-white.

O'Keeffe had pronounced them "just what I need," and said, "You will do the developing for the rest of the month."

Parker had laughed but smothered his reaction when he caught sight of her stern face in the light of the kerosene lantern. "Here," she'd said, "is a book of instructions if you have any questions. Read it tonight. Next I'll show you how I want frames made for my canvases and how to tack the fabric to them just right." She looked at the web of strings and all the new negatives.

"I don't usually take on studio assistants, Parker," she said, "but I spent a few years, back there, sick, and in the hospital. I need to have a good showing from this year to prove I'm still . . . O'Keeffe." She cleared her throat. "Enough of that."

Parker smiled. At least now he knew why she wanted him to hang around. It clearly wasn't for conversation or friendship. The dude ranch already had plenty of gardeners and cooks and house-keepers for her to order around. His only purpose was to develop photographs, and it paid him in three meals a day. All he had to do was be quiet around this strange character and let her "paint."

"Oh, look," she said now, as they whipped around the corner to the dirt road. Parker grabbed the door handle and stared down the road at a line of sheep.

"Is there a shepherd with them?" O'Keeffe shaded her eyes for a better view. "Perhaps that Santo Domingo boy who helped you in the desert? William Dark Sky?" She stepped on the brake.

"Cain't rightly tell from here."

"Go see," she said. "If it's him, tell him to take a message back to his Pueblo. I want more of that little Clara Dark Sky's pottery. He can take their Kachina dolls back, too."

"Dolls?" Parker tried to imagine William playing with dolls. They had to belong to his sister.

"They're not actually playthings," she said. "Well, they are, after a fashion. They are models for children of the tribe's spirit dancers."

"Is there a ram spirit?" Parker interrupted.

"I don't know. Now, get out and see if that is your William. You know where to find me." Parker nodded. The next thing he knew, he was waving at a cloud of dust.

He walked for five minutes before he could see that the Indian was William. He cursed himself for forgetting to bring water along. He should have known by now. Everything looked closer than it really was here.

"Hello?" he yelled loudly. *"Hello?"* echoed back at him from the colored cliff. Parker swung around to look back at the outcrop. It seemed for a moment that all its colors were melting together in the hot sunshine. He stared. Nothing moved while he watched, of course. He breathed easier, but he could see how dust from the crumbly gray rocks on top was sliding downward onto the next layer. Some of the cream color streaked down over the red layer. Rains had washed all the layers down, staining one another. In fact, Parker realized, the rocky outcropping was actually melting, only very, very slowly, rain by rain. O'Keeffe had seen it. And, as poor a painter as she was, she had shown him.

"You are well, Parker?" William hiked up to him. "That is good."

Parker turned, looked into the Indian's eyes, and remembered the blessed canteen full of water. Suddenly he did not know what to say to William. It wasn't a feeling he was used to, but then, he told himself, he'd never had his life saved before. He gestured at the sheep, and stared at the ram that led the little flock. "I hate woolies," he said, "but that is one fine ram."

"We care for one another," William said. "They are family."

"Oh," Parker did not understand, but he nodded anyway. "O'Keeffe says that your sister can come get the dolls whenever she wants. And she wants her to bring another pot."

Now William nodded. He seemed to be waiting for something.

"I guess I should say some sort of thanks," Parker mumbled.

"You still see spirits."

"Heck, no," Parker reassured him. "I am fine now. You did just right by me with all that water. And then getting me to O'Keeffe's. Thank you," he repeated. Parker shifted from foot to foot. "I reckon I better be getting back to her now," he said.

William nodded. "She still has much to give you."

"Yes, well." Parker thought. Carrot juice? "She does feed me. And she wants a pot, now. Don't you forget."

"Yes," William said.

Yes? Parker thought. He gave a half wave and headed back toward the colored cliffs. He felt the hairs on his arms stir. Strange character, he told himself, and walked faster. He made a note not to be there when William brought his sister's pottery to O'Keeffe.

As he crossed the road, a car pulled up. A woman in a bright red hat leaned out the window. "Young man?" she warbled. "Yoo-hoo, young man!"

Parker went over. "Yes, ma'am?"

"Does this road take us to where we can see Miss O'Keeffe paint?"

"She doesn't even let *me* watch her paint," he said.

"Yes, but is this where she is working?"

Parker stared at the women in the car behind the driver. They looked rich and hot, and their accents came from back East. "Are you friends of hers?" Parker asked them.

"Oh, mercy me, *no*," the woman gushed. "*Us* know Georgia O'Keeffe? We just want to *watch* her for a bit, isn't that right, girls? Maybe get our *picture* taken with her." There was a chorus of giggles from the backseat.

Parker thought quickly. "I don't rightly know where *Miss* O'Keeffe is working right this moment, but there is a real, live Indian down that way with a herd of sheep." He pointed toward where William had walked. "Very photogenic. And he could tell you where to go for Indian pots."

"Oooh, thank you *so* very much," the woman said. Parker winced as the transmission ground into gear and their car took off.

Parker smiled and headed toward the cliff.

"O'Keeffe?" he said quietly, near the car. "Excuse me, but . . ." O'Keeffe held her hand out to silence him. She was dabbing a deep blue green at the painting, making tiny specks of color at the top. Parker looked up at the cliff. The specks were the bushes up there, he realized, tiny because they were far away. He looked back at the painting in surprise. They looked real now, following the line of the cliff's edge.

O'Keeffe took a breath. Parker realized he'd been holding his, too.

She patted her brush back into a gob of green on the glass palette, and then smeared a bit of yellow in. Next she dabbed more tiny specks to show the brush growing in the cracks of the cliff. As her brush got closer to the bottom of the canvas, the bush splotches got bigger. At the very bottom, she took more time, adding scratchy details and mixing dark purple into the green for shadows.

She took a step backward and turned on him. "Now," she said sharply. "What is so all-fired important that you would dare—?"

"I just steered some folks away. Did you ask some ladies out here to watch you paint?"

"Ha!" she hooted. "You know just how likely that is. I can't be bothered to be polite to all of them."

"All of them?"

"Fans," she said flatly. "I don't know how they find me. Once a woman knocked on my door and swore she'd come a thousand miles to 'see Miss O'Keeffe.' I suppose she thought I was the maid." Her eyes twinkled. "Well, I just posed pretty and said, 'Front view,' then turned around and said, 'Back view.' Then I said, 'Good-bye' and closed the door in her face." Parker was laughing along with her when she looked over his shoulder and gasped, "Oh, no . . ."

Another car had pulled up by the dry water trough. A fat man stepped out and walked around to open the passenger door. "Oooh," a woman squealed. "It's Miss O'Keeffe herself!" She jumped out and started running toward the painter, but her high heels caught in the sand.

Fans, Parker thought. Fans of what?

"You take care of them," O'Keeffe told Parker, and turned back to the painting.

"They aren't friends of yours?"

She snorted.

"Welcome," Parker said loudly. He spread his hands as he walked toward the couple. "I am afraid you good folks are mistaken. That is not Miss O'Keeffe." He helped the woman to her feet. "That is just my, um, Aunt Merita."

The woman craned her neck, trying to see past Parker. "It looked like Georgia O'Keeffe," she said. She stared harder. "No, I see you are right. Your aunt is much skinnier than Miss O'Keeffe."

Parker said, "So, tell me about this Georgia O'Keeffe." He walked with them back to the car.

"Oh," the woman said. "Don't you know? She's just the most famous woman painter in the world."

"She sells her paintings for tens of thousands of dollars," the man panted. "Though I can't see much in them. They're 'modern art,' my Mildred says." Parker noticed that his face was red and he was sweating hard.

"It *is* modern," the woman said. "Georgia O'Keeffe was on the cover of *Life* magazine last year, Bertrand; don't you remember?" She turned back to stare at the woman holding the palette. "You sure that's not her?"

"Like I said," Parker repeated, "that's my Aunt Merita. Her paintings aren't modern and I wouldn't give a wooden nickel for them, if you know what I mean." He winked. Parker opened the woman's door and waited. When she did not move, he said, "Aunt Merita likes me to stay near while she works so I can chase away the rattlesnakes." The woman jumped into the car.

"They don't bite much," Parker reassured her. "It's the scorpions you have to watch out for."

He chucked and waved as the car sped down the road. Parker walked back to O'Keeffe, thinking, World famous? The cover of a magazine? Thousands of dollars for a painting? He stared at O'Keeffe.

"Did you tell anyone where I was painting?" she demanded when he got back. Parker shrugged and shook his head no. "Well, *someone* did. Some fans would pay to know where I am working." She shoved her glass palette back into its box. "The word is out now. You will drive us back." She jammed the paintbrushes, still wet, into a can and slammed the car door.

"How dare they?" She was still steaming as Parker climbed behind the wheel. "It must have been that Merita! She knew where the skull was. *She* must have given people directions." He started the car, thinking about O'Keeffe and her fans. "You just wait," the world's most famous woman painter went on, "till I give that Merita a piece of my mind."

Parker just kept driving. There was plenty of time, he knew, for her anger to wear off before they reached the Ghost Ranch. Finally, her tirade was over. "O'Keeffe," he began, "those fans of yours . . ."

"Oh, yes," she said. "Do tell what you said to make them scurry away so fast. I looked back, and that man's face was positively green!"

CHAPTER NINE

Kachina

Parker sat on a stool in the studio and watched silently as O'Keeffe tapped the canvas he'd stretched over a new frame. "Tight as a drum." She nodded in approval and brushed it with white paint. Parker had nothing else to do but watch. There were no photographs to develop. All of the brushes had been soaked in turpentine, wiped on cloths, washed in soap and water, rinsed well, and set carefully to dry. "I am very particular about my tools," she had said when she first explained their care. Then she had winked at him and said, "Mostly, I am just particular, hmmm?"

Now she turned back to her melted-mountain painting. It stood on an easel, along with one of the pictures she had taken of the hill. She peered at the photo, then stepped back and studied her painting.

Parker yawned. He got up and ambled over to the stack of paintings leaning, face against the wall, in the corner of the room. He figured there had to be more than twenty there.

"The kachina paintings," O'Keeffe said. "Pull them out. In case

Clara comes for her dolls today." She gestured at a row of small wooden dolls standing on a shelf built into the adobe wall. Some had antlers or horns on top. Others wore strange markings on their faces. None of them looked like real people—and certainly none looked like a baby doll fit for a little girl to play with.

Parker began tilting up the paintings, one by one. He'd seen them before, but, to his surprise, sheets of heavy paper lay between some of the oil paintings on canvas—paper with black-and-white pencil drawings or ones of smudgy black. There were trees and roads, adobe buildings, cliffs, and churches; but O'Keeffe had drawn them all as simple shapes without details. They were nothing, Parker decided, he would ever have looked at before he knew O'Keeffe.

There. He pulled out a half a handful of stiff papers. On each was a painting of one of the kachinas. He held them up. "These?" he asked.

"Stand them up so I can see them," she instructed.

Parker spread them out on the windowsills and table. "Don't touch those leaves!" O'Keeffe scolded as he moved to brush them away. He sighed and worked the display around the reddish brown leaves, the paint chips, the goat's skull, and the odd round rocks she was always bringing back from her walks in the desert. "Now stand out of the way."

Parker backed off and watched as she studied her paintings. A child, he thought, could have done half of them. One, with the doll painted to fill nearly the whole space, made the kachina look solemn and important. Another one, obviously a mistake, showed only the top of the doll's head in the bottom left corner of the space with one feather drooping over its eye. It made no sense to Parker. He watched the artist gather the pile of them together. On the back of a few paintings, she wrote something big. He stepped closer. It was a star with the letters *O'K* inside. "You never sign your paintings on the front, do you?" he asked. O'Keeffe didn't answer, but put the kachina paintings in a pile on the windowsill.

An airplane engine roared overhead, so low that Parker ducked. He grinned at her. "Never got used to the noise myself," she said, and turned back to her new white painting. "Oh," she said after a few brushstrokes, "perhaps my package came in Arthur's plane. Go see. And I have some letters to send over to Phoebe at the main house in time for today's mail." She opened a drawer and gave him a handful.

He was out the door before she could say any more. The Ghost Ranch's owner had let him touch his plane's propellers once. Parker could not imagine how rich someone would have to be to have a real airplane. Arthur Pack looked and talked like a normal man, but he owned the ranch with all the cows and horses, all the casitas, the cliffs and dry riverbed, a tractor, an automobile, and an airplane, too. O'Keeffe didn't seem impressed at all. Parker wished he could tell his ma and pa about it.

Even when times had been good at the farm, they had no extras. Parker walked toward the main house, thinking. Pa had always thanked God to have enough food on the table, though. Parker's mouth watered, remembering the farm meals: fried steak and red-eye gravy, fresh biscuits, corn and beans, and for dessert, Ma's apple pie. That was before the drought hit and pickings got so slim. That was long before Pa had finally gone away looking for work. Then times really got bad. "Hard times, everywhere," Ma always said. Parker thought she had probably never seen anything like the Ghost Ranch. Somehow there didn't seem to be any "Great Depression" here at all. Parker wondered if Mr. Pack ever thanked God for his airplane.

That made him realize he hadn't thanked God for anything in a long time.

"Hey, Dust Boy!" Clyde sauntered out of the main house, followed by a young Indian. "Got you a new girl here, fresh from the Santo Domingo Pueblo."

Parker guessed the youngster was eleven or twelve years old. That was about the age his sister would have been, he realized, but this girl was nothing like Sally Belle. The Indian had dark skin and darker hair, tied at her neck, and wore a long heavy skirt. She stared at the ground, looking angry. Parker struggled to remember what William had called his sister. "Clara?" he called. She looked up, her eyes bright with relief.

"Miss O'Keeffe has your dollies, right?" She looked confused, so he said, louder, "Your dolls? Your kachinas?" Finally the girl nodded. "Your brother told me you were coming, so they're ready."

"My brother?" Clara's voice was little more than a whisper.

"William Dark Sky." Parker could not believe how slow this girl was. "The shepherd? Your brother?"

"Come on, Parker," Clyde interrupted. "What do you expect? She's just a dumb Indian. Mr. Pack told me to walk her over to O'Keeffe's casita, probably so she wouldn't steal anything on the way." He winked. "You can take her from here."

"I have to check for the mail." Parker waved the handful of O'Keeffe's letters.

"You cain't be thinking to take *her* into the main house with you." Clyde leered at the girl, and she stepped closer to Parker.

"Yep," Parker said, stunned by how familiar it seemed to have a little girl shadowing him. Sally Belle had done that. He swallowed.

"Strangest taste I ever saw in sweethearts," Clyde hooted. "Wait till the other hands hear about this!"

"You can just crawl back under your rock, Clyde. Clara is here on business with O'Keeffe." Parker headed for the main house with Clara in tow. "Did you bring the pottery for O'Keeffe?" he asked as they walked.

"What pottery?"

"Didn't William tell you?" he asked. Clara stared at him, her dark eyes wide. Parker shook his head, wondering why he was trying to hold a conversation with an Indian.

"'Morning, Miz Phoebe." He tipped his hat to the owner's girlfriend.

Phoebe Pack glanced down at Clara. Her mouth tightened. "Arthur and I told your family to set up their camp down the road, didn't we? And not to pester our guests to buy souvenirs from you?"

"I have business with the lady artist," Clara said.

Phoebe nodded and took O'Keeffe's mail from Parker. "Package by the cottonwood," she said.

Parker hurried out of the adobe house onto the patio. A huge cottonwood grew right within the wall. In the dust-dry soil at its base sat a cardboard box tied up with string and a bundle of letters. Parker smiled down at the little girl and picked up the package. "Tell me about your dollies," he said as they turned toward O'Keeffe's casita.

"They're not dollies," she said firmly.

"No offense," Parker said, hiding a smile. "I know they're not exactly toys. They're kachinas, right?" Clara was silent. Parker tried again. "Maybe you could tell me the difference?"

"My uncle carved them for me himself, from the roots of cottonwood trees."

"Is that kind of wood special?" Parker prompted. He longed for the feel of a little girl's hand in his again. He clenched the package more tightly.

"The cottonwood roots always know where to reach for water," Clara explained, "even if there is no rain."

"I wish for rain all the time." Parker cleared his throat, then tried to keep his voice steady. "My life was good until the drought began." He fought down a flood of memories of his family—and Sally Belle playing with a cornhusk doll he had made for her. "If those kachina things aren't for playing," he asked Clara, "why do you keep them?"

"They are to remember by."

"To remember what?" Parker asked.

"The gods. The spirits."

"Oh, kachinas are old Indian superstitions, right?"

"No." Clara stopped walking. "Our spirits are real. And they are now, like Jesus and your saints. You have kachinas of them, don't you? I've seen them in the mission church."

Parker opened his mouth, then closed it. Ma had kept a crucifix on the wall back at home. Was that a kachina? It certainly was not a doll. Clara, he decided, was smarter than she looked. "You're right," he finally said. "They're not toys." They started walking again.

"The kachinas my uncle made for me are like my guardian spirits. I keep them hanging on my wall or from my ceiling. Some kachinas bring rain. Others make the crops grow. Many others keep life going in our village. I look at them and feel safe." Parker dashed away a memory of Sally Belle talking about her guardian angel. "Our spirit gods have power," Clara said. "But some of them are playful, too."

Parker pictured the little wooden dolls on their shelf. They didn't look like guardian angels—and they didn't look very powerful, either. Then he remembered the kachina paintings that O'Keeffe had signed. One had made a doll fill the page, commanding all the space to itself. It surely looked powerful that way. The other painting had shown a doll scurrying away, as playfully as any pixie. She must have actually felt the spirits behind the kachinas. Then she'd caught them in paint for anyone to see—anyone willing to look through her eyes.

"I'll feel better when I get them back," Clara said. "I shouldn't have loaned kachinas to anybody."

Parker led Clara into the casita and dropped the package and mail on a low table. O'Keeffe was facing the white canvas, staring from ram's skull to leaves and back again in silence. He could not help wondering if she was seeing spirits there, too. He stared at the leaves.

"Put those down!" O"Keeffe's voice made him jump. "Did you ask permission to look at my paintings?"

"No." Clara stood in the corner, holding a canvas.

"She didn't mean any harm," Parker said.

"Was I speaking to you?" O'Keeffe asked sharply.

"No, ma'am," Parker said, "but Clara was just—"

"No one sees my work until I feel it is done," she said. Parker thought of all the times he'd looked over her shoulder. She had to have known he was peeking, yet she'd allowed him to look, and she'd told him to go through that pile this very morning. Nothing the woman did made any sense.

"Take your kachinas and go," O'Keeffe said, turning back to the canvas.

Clara looked at Parker. He took the dolls off the shelf and handed them to her with a shrug. He followed the girl out into the hot sunshine. "That wasn't fair," Parker fumed. "There was no reason for her to treat you that way."

"She enters a trance to work," Clara said. She didn't seem upset at all. "I have spoken to her before, at better times." She waved good-bye and went down the road.

A trance? Parker thought, as he reentered the casita. That was one way of looking at it. A Jesus kachina? A guardian spirit? Gods? Clara had strange thoughts on normal things. And she sounded so sure of herself. Were all Indians this religious? Was Sally Belle?

"Clara was supposed to bring me a pot," O'Keeffe said. "Where *is* it?"

"I don't know," Parker snapped. Would she have treated Sally

Belle like this, he wondered. No please or thank you—not ever. Was she above everyday courtesy? Finally his thoughts burst out loud. "Just because you're an artist and all famous," Parker ranted, "there's no call to be mean to a sweet little girl."

O'Keeffe looked stricken. "Go, find her and apologize for me," she said, then turned back to her painting. "And tell her I want that pottery."

CHAPTER TEN

Mirage

Parker covered half the driveway before he realized he was leaving. He looked back toward the Ghost Ranch, but it was already hidden below a rise. I arrived with nothing, he thought. Put in my time. Got paid in food. His legs swung easily, eating up the distance toward the dirt road. Don't owe anybody anything, he told himself.

He decided to turn west, toward California, whistling to himself as he walked along through the crisp morning air. When he heard the crunching sound of an automobile behind him, he didn't break stride. It might be a ride, he thought, or somebody else who needed a few days' work. He'd know how to handle them as soon as he'd sized them up. Unless it was somebody like O'Keeffe, who didn't fit any pat- tern. Or a sidewinder like Clyde. He glanced back over his shoulder.

It was the Ghost Ranch car. Parker looked for cover, then realized that the automobile was moving too cautiously to be driven by Clyde. It pulled up beside him, and Phoebe Pack leaned out the window.

"That you, Parker?" she called. "I'm headed over to Abiquiu, and I could use a hand. Got a minute?"

Parker thought fast. "Sure thing, Miz Phoebe." He pictured the little town huddled around its church. Maybe somebody there could use a worker for a day. He walked around the car and opened the passenger door. Bundles of cloth fell out.

"Goodness!" Phoebe laughed. "Just throw them into the back." As Parker made space to sit, she explained, "These clothes are for the nuns to share with the village folks and the Indians nearby." She shifted smoothly and headed down the road.

"Ma used to give to the poor, too," Parker said.

"Well, God bless her," Phoebe said. "My guests are all good that way, too, sharing the wealth."

"Not O'Keeffe," Parker guessed.

"Oh, yes. She's a character, but underneath everything, she's a good woman. O'Keeffe gives clothes and money, too, especially to the school up here." Parker shook his head, unwilling to believe.

"You only have one more week left of your sentence, don't you? You were very lucky O'Keeffe was willing to strike a bargain with the sheriff. We've had so many thefts this past year. Hard times truly test people." She sighed. "Many fail."

Parker was glad he hadn't mentioned California. The sheriff would be after him if anybody knew he'd failed O'Keeffe and left for good. Or maybe he'd failed Sheriff Young, he thought, and probably his ma and pa, too. Parker felt sick to his stomach.

"Strong young fellow like you ought to be signing up for the Civilian Conservation Corps," Phoebe was saying. "After your sentence is served, of course. It's an honest way to make money."

Money sounded good. "What is it?" Parker asked.

"Oh, President Roosevelt is putting hundreds of thousands of young men to work, building roads and such in national parks and around. The CCC means hard labor, but steady money, I've heard tell. It's good to have honest work to do, even in a depression."

Phoebe fell silent as she eased the car up the steep hill into town and through narrow streets between adobe houses. Parker thought about the CCC. If he got to California and found his pa, he wouldn't need to look for a job. It rained in California and fields grew lush with crops. He and Pa could start up a new farm if—the thought chilled him—he could find Pa. It would help if he'd sent any letters home after he'd left. Parker stared through the window. They had never heard from Pa at all. Had he failed, too?

Parker made himself look at the village. Tiny gardens peeked green from behind dirt walls, and he realized there had to be a spring in the town, and irrigation ditches. There was water here, even in the middle of the desert, he thought—if you knew where to look for it.

"Here," Phoebe said. "Follow me." Parker grabbed two of the biggest bundles and trailed her to a small building behind the main adobe church.

"Oh, *gracias!*" a slender little nun said, opening the door. Her long black habit swept the dusty ground as she turned to let them into the cool, shadowy room. There was almost no furniture inside, but a large wooden crucifix hung on the wall. Parker stared at it a moment. It was clearly hand carved, and he wondered if it was made from cottonwood roots. It housed a powerful spirit, he thought. *"Por favor."* The nun smiled and pointed to the corner. Parker set his bundle down next to Phoebe's and headed out for more. Three trips later, the car was empty, and the nun brought them glasses of cool water and jelly-smeared bread. *"Gracias, gracias,"* she repeated over and over, shaking their hands and smiling widely.

"Do you want a ride back to the ranch now?" Phoebe asked.

Parker looked away. "I have to be looking for Clara and her family," he said.

"Try over toward the Chama River," Phoebe suggested.

As soon as Phoebe's car had turned the corner, he headed out, away from the river.

Down the hill from the village and away from the road, the desert was quiet. Midday heat shimmered over the plains. Parker walked toward a row of cottonwoods in the distance. He could hope for a stream there, but even shade would be a relief. Sunlight seemed to vibrate, hovering above the sagebrush and creosote bushes. Parker stared at it until his eyes watered. Hints of blue and pink, gray-green and tan rippled through the light. He blinked at the mirage, now seeming to be a full-blown lake lying in the lowlands in front of the cottonwoods. Parker strode on toward it, knowing there was no water but that California lay somewhere in that direction; California and his father.

As the sun rose, Parker began to wish he'd brought a canteen along. His stomach growled warningly. At last he neared the cottonwoods. The trees seemed to be growing down in a gully. "The roots know where to find water," Clara had said. He hoped she was right. Walking silently to the edge of the cut, he looked down through the branches. Ten feet below him, a mule deer buck lay resting beside a trickle of water.

Parker held his breath. The buck's big ears flicked as if to shoo flies, but he did not seem to know he was being watched. Parker could see the animal's sides swelling with each gentle breath and its eyelashes, stiff and long against his cheeks. Now and then the animal burped and slowly chewed its cud. Like a cow, Parker thought. He wondered how long it had been since he'd tasted fresh venison but, mouth watering, soon gave up. Without a gun, there was no need to torture himself. Parker smiled. If he could somehow kill the buck, he would make sure to thank the deer's spirit for making it possible.

A sudden shriek from a jay made him jump. The buck leaped to its feet and stood trembling as the jay called again. The deer's ears swiveled wildly, listening for the source of danger. He raised his nose to sniff the air and froze at the sight of Parker overhead.

Fear held the animal only for a heartbeat. Then it was off, scrambling up the far side of the cut, his sharp hooves scraping and sliding, then catching in the soft dry soil. The buck heaved itself over the edge and bounded off, stiff legged, zigzagging across the desert toward California. Parker watched him through the treetops, then finally eased himself over the edge and slithered down the bank toward the tiny creek.

He leaned down, cupping his hands in the flow, waiting for a mouthful to gather before he drank. The water tasted muddy, but Parker didn't much care. It was wet. He wiped his face with his damp hands and gathered another helping from the trickle. Over and over, he scooped up mouthfuls of water.

"Parker," a voice over him said. "You would be easy to ambush."

"William!" Parker stood up and looked straight into the sun. He put up a hand to block the worst of the glare. The boy stood on the edge of the gully, leaning on his long staff. Beside him a row of curious sheep looked down. One bleated a quiet *baaaa*. The ram was there, too, his horns looking twisted and dangerous. Parker shuddered. "Follow the water that way." William pointed downstream.

While the Indian and his flock walked along above, Parker dodged tree trunks and fallen rocks. At last the gully widened, and its banks spread into gentle slopes. At William's urging, the sheep hitched their way down, toward the water. Soon a dozen woolly animals pushed against one another, fighting to shove their muzzles into the water. The streambed filled with slurps and snorts, baa-ing, and the squishy sounds of hooves in mud. Parker grinned at William. "Yum," he said.

William nodded. The sheep drank their fill, then settled down to nibble grasses. "Did you see the deer?" Parker asked.

"Yes," William said. "It is a good sign."

More superstitions, of course, Parker thought. "Did you remember to ask Clara to make some pottery for O'Keeffe?" he asked. There was no answer. He tried again. "Did those tourists find you?"

"They could not," William said quietly. There was no way to have a normal conversation with any Indian, Parker thought, except Clara. She could talk a mean streak once she got started. He watched as William moved upstream several paces, then bent and dug deeply into the streambed with his hands. He settled his canteen pot in and waited for it to fill.

Afternoon thunder rumbled in the distance. "I hope one of these storms drops rain on us soon," Parker said. He wondered if he'd get more attention if he just said *baaaa* like one of the sheep. To his surprise, William answered.

"There is enough water here," he said. "And rain will come soon enough. The deer spirit, Soi'ngwa, is a rain bringer. He has shown himself." He picked up his staff. "Walk with us?" Without pausing for an answer, he clambered up the slope. His sheep followed. The tardy ones got a hurry-along tap from William's long stick.

Parker and William meandered along at sheep speed, pausing to graze here, cantering ahead in mock fright there. They talked all afternoon, about Parker's family, about the airplane, about O'Keeffe. Sometimes Parker even got an answer. More often, he was just left thinking over the things he'd said.

"That hill yonder," he said presently. "That's the one that O'Keeffe painted, only we're coming at it from the back, right?" There was no answer from William. His sheep spread out to munch on a spread of dry grasses. "I'm going to go and look at the melting cliff," Parker said. "Will you be here awhile?" He waited for an answer, then said, "Well, then I'll find you back here, I suppose."

Parker jogged around the hill and stared up at the colors shifting down the cliff. In real life, it was just like O'Keeffe had shown. So were the kachinas. O'Keeffe, he decided, was a very good painter, in her own way. He shook his head, thinking about how she'd treated Clara.

The clattering sound of horses' hooves filtered into his attention. Parker turned to see who was coming. It was the painter herself. She cantered up and swung off the horse. "Parker," she said. Then she stared at the hillside. "Look at that light. I'll have to paint it again. I do that, you know, trying until I get it right."

"Howdy, O'Keeffe," Parker said, trying to shame her for not even saying hi.

She didn't seem to notice. "I was out on my evening rounds," she told him. "I thought you might have come here." Parker blinked, but the artist was reaching back toward the horse's saddle. "I brought you a canteen of water and a blanket. You hungry?"

Parker was too surprised to answer. "Here." She swung a lunch pail to him and a camera, too. He took them without thinking. "You've got a good eye, Parker," she said. "See what it looks like here tomorrow morning"—she gestured at the cliff—"and, when you get home, we'll see if I should try painting it in dawn light."

O'Keeffe turned to look at the cliff one more time, then turned and mounted her horse. "Stay safe," she said, and cantered back toward the Ghost Ranch.

CHAPTER ELEVEN

White

Parker had trouble sleeping that night. He scolded himself for getting soft. He had slept out on the road before, but things were different, then—simpler. Once he rolled out of the blanket onto the sandy dirt. Shivering, he brushed the sand off his cheek and rolled up again, glad for the scratchy warmth of tightly woven wool. He thought to thank the sheep for its wool, which led him to wonder about spirits.

Another time, the call of coyotes echoing against the cliff came so close he thought they were going to attack him. Parker pressed back into the shelter of the juniper bush and tried to be silent while his heart pounded. He listened to the coyote's calls change suddenly, then relaxed as their excited yips chased some prey off into the darkness. Finally he heard a gurgling scream as their hunt ended. Drought meant hard times for the coyotes, too.

Once, he awoke to rustling sounds nearby. Starshine and moonlight were bright enough to cast shadows, but not bright enough to show him what all was slithering and skittering along on the ground nearby. Parker pulled the blanket tighter and tried to will himself back to sleep. That was hard, with O'Keeffe's surprise visit running through his mind. This wasn't fair, he thought. His decision had been made. He was going to California. Now he had to stay and take pictures at dawn for a crazy artist who couldn't say please. Had he been trapped? If he had, at least he'd been fed and covered, too. It gave him a nice feeling to think of her turning on horseback and telling him to stay safe. As soon as he settled back into sleep, his eyes opened to make sure he hadn't missed dawn's colors reflecting against the cliff.

At last the sky paled to charcoal gray, then blue seeped into the shadows. At the first sign of gold by the horizon, Parker unrolled himself and got stiffly to his feet. He checked the film in O'Keeffe's camera, ate a last biscuit from the pail, stretched, and groaned. The glittering orange rimmed a cloudless sky. Parker peered through the lens at the cliff. Every one of its rock layers had changed color. He snapped the shutter and wound the film. Moving sideways, he retraced the route O'Keeffe had taken that first day, snapping shots as the pinks deepened to orange, the buff became peach, and the white rock became flesh.

Suddenly Parker let the camera sag against his chest. "Stupid," he yelled to the desert. "*Stupid!*" the cliff yelled back. "Black and white!" he told the desert. "Photos are black and white." He let himself crumple to his knees.

What kind of fool was he? "You have a good eye," O'Keeffe had said. What good was an eye if there were no brains attached? How— Parker gazed at the cliff before him—was he supposed to catch the dawn colors in black and white?

He looked up at the rocks and tried to see the darkest parts as black. Bright sun on the white rock bands would be as close to white as the film would record. Between was gray, of course—but how many tones of gray there were! He stared at the shadows cast by pinnacles and then, darker still, hidden within rock clefts. They had all moved since dawn's first light.

He picked up the camera again and went back by the bush. He tried to hit all the spots he'd shot before and took new photos where the brights and deep shadows had moved the most. Another perfect contrast appeared as light struck the tip of a boulder hidden inside a shady hole. It got easier. As Parker moved around the cliff now, he didn't see the pink and orange of the rocks, the turquoise of the sky, or the deep greens of the junipers. They all were pales against darks, white against rich grays, black and white in pattern.

Too soon, the roll of film was done. Parker sighed and looked around. The sky was bright blue, but the whiteness of the first cloud against it was a sharp contrast. The ground was still tan, but each little cactus cast a dark shadow. And there, there, and *there*— coyote tracks collected their own dark shadows in the slanted sun light. The tracks were everywhere, now that he was looking at the ground this way.

Parker yawned. He wandered back to the rug under the spruce and lay down, exhausted. "I got your photographs, O'Keeffe," he grumbled aloud. "Can I go to California now?" Parker drank deeply from the canteen. He stretched out on his back and threw an arm over his eyes against the rising sun. The decision could wait. Sleep came first.

Parker awoke to the deafening croak of a raven on a juniper branch by his head. He sat up quickly, and a black vulture launched into flight from the ground nearby. It joined two others circling in the midday sun. "Forget it, fellas!" He waved his arms at them.

He shook out the blanket. "Whoops!" Parker cried, and dived for the photograph of his family. He dusted it off and cradled it in his hands, staring intently. He'd been lying on it; that was clear from the fold and a scratch across the sky over the roof of the farm-house. Parker sighed. He looked so young in the picture. And Sally Belle had just lost her first tooth. He brushed his finger across his mother's face, barely touching the photograph. Parker had to clear his throat before he could ask, "What should I do, Ma?"

He could leave the camera, the blanket and pail by the tree. O'Keeffe would know where to look for them. Ma would probably have liked O'Keeffe, Parker thought. She'd be right proud to know that a real artist had told him he had a good eye.

He tried looking at the photo with his good eye, and it seemed different, somehow. Everybody looked so stiff, posed staring at the camera in their Sunday best. If he had taken the picture, Parker thought, he'd have taken off Pa's tie and his jacket, too. Maybe he'd even have put a bottle in Pa's hand. The idea startled him, but it seemed the only way to catch Pa's spirit. Parker would be standing as tall as he could with Pa's arm draped over his shoulders, loving and maybe leaning a little, too.

To stop that thought, Parker stared at his sister. Sally Belle had never sat still on chairs like that, her back stiff and straight. She should be kneeling in the field, building a playhouse of grass for her cornhusk dolls. Her hair would be loose, blowing like corn silk in the wind. Parker decided that Ma would be sitting on a threadbare quilt with an open book nearby. Her arms would be full of fresh-picked wildflowers, and even her eyes would be smiling.

Parker realized he was smiling, too. That was how it should be, he thought. He wished he could go back and take a photograph that showed how his family was—brave and hopeful, poor as they were.

Parker looked at the camera and sighed. He carefully slid the photograph into his shirt pocket and gathered O'Keeffe's things. Then he began the walk back to the Ghost Ranch.

Parker heard the supper bell as he turned into the ranch's long driveway. His stomach had rumbled along all afternoon, but he was too dusty to arrive at the table without washing first. He paused to drain the last of the canteen's water. Then he shouldered his bundles again and headed for the casita.

Its door stood open, welcoming him. The skulls and smooth desert stones O'Keeffe had gathered sat gleaming in the last sunshine. Parker grinned, deciding to surprise her. He set the blanket and camera on the adobe bench and walked in silently. The sharp, rich smell of fresh oil paints engulfed him at the door.

When he saw the painting, he could only stop and stare. The ram's skull floated high in a sky, its rough horns smoothed out to look like wings or worshipful arms cupped heavenward. Somehow she had painted the skull itself to look directly at the viewer even though it had no eyes. Shivers ran down Parker's spine as he realized how close she'd come to painting his hallucination.

O'Keeffe had painted the leaves huge as boulders beneath the skull. The leaves' veins looked like the shadowy channels that water carved into the desert wherever it passed. Red-brown, black, and cream: All of the colors matched the cliffs and mesas of the Ghost Ranch. Dead leaves and a dead skull—and yet they were so alive!

He studied the background. It was not flat after all. O'Keeffe had worked a blue paint in to shimmer through the white. There were pale greens, dusty tan, and pinks, too. The whole background seemed to shift as Parker looked at it. A mirage, he thought. O'Keeffe had managed to paint the heat shimmering in the desert distance. He shook his head. She'd done it all in only two days. Of course, he reminded himself, she'd been studying the pieces and paint patches for weeks, thinking and planning.

"Sick, ain't it?" Clyde's voice stunned Parker. He whirled about.

"What are you doing here?" Parker demanded. "Where is O'Keeffe?"

"Easy," Clyde crooned. "She is over at the dining hall, laughing and eating nice and normal. There ain't nothing to get all hot about, except . . ." He pointed at the painting.

"What's wrong with the painting?" Parker asked.

"Ha!" Clyde hooted. Then he looked closely at Parker's face. "You don't see it, do you? Look again, sucker. It's a woman's privates, all leafy outside and little tunnels inside." Clyde stopped. "You don't see it 'cause you never been there, have you?"

Parker flushed. "That's not fair. I—I—" He stumbled into silence.

"You never even seen a *picture* of a lady's parts?" Clyde chuckled darkly. "Well, that's the kind of thing this painter is known for."

Parker tried not to turn back to look at the painting, but he had to. He could almost see what Clyde was talking about, parts he'd seen in cows birthing and pigs at slaughter. That could be the same in a woman. He tried not to believe it of O'Keeffe, but once that idea was in his head, he could hardly see the ram's spirit staring straight at him from the middle of the canvas. Parker's chest felt tight. "She's not like that," he said.

"All women are"—Clyde made a slow, sly wink—"once you get to know them."

"You're wrong," Parker shot back.

"But you're not sure, are you?"

Parker stared at the ranch hand's handsome face and felt his fists curl at his sides. "Does O'Keeffe know you're in here?" he demanded.

"Naw. Does she know *you're* in here?"

"Uh, no," Parker said. "Not for certain."

"Well then," Clyde said quickly. He flashed a wide smile. "We're even. I won't tell that you were sneaking around in here if you keep quiet about me. I was just checking on things, looking for mice. What's your story going to be?" Laughing, he left—just as the ranch generator switched off and the lights went out.

CHAPTER TWELVE

Black

By the time O'Keeffe returned from supper, Parker had stumbled about in the black casita, found the lanterns, and lit them. His face and hands were washed, and he'd changed back into his clothes. He had helped himself to slice after slice of bread and most of a jar of honey. What he had not done was look at the newest painting.

"You're back," O'Keeffe said, striding through the door. "Did the cliff look different at dawn?"

Parker almost laughed. No howdy, no welcome home, no how are you? At least, there were no surprises. Except in her paintings. O'Keeffe stared at him. "Parker?" she asked. "What's wrong?"

He gestured at the ram's skull canvas.

"I think it turned out rather nicely, don't you?" She studied the painting by lantern light. "I'll work it over for a few more days, of course. The line isn't quite right here yet." Her finger traced the bottom edge of the ram's right horn.

"What is it?" Parker asked.

"Cobalt blue against titanium white and raw . . ." Her voice broke off. "That's not what you mean, is it?" She looked at his face. "It is a ram's skull with brown leaves. It is the entire desert in three objects."

"And the mirage floating behind them," Parker added.

O'Keeffe nodded. "Exactly." But as Parker looked, he could see the other meaning, just as clearly, in her painting. He tried to think how to ask her without letting her know that Clyde had been in her casita, leering at her painting.

"A fellow could see other things there," he said, and felt his face flush.

"Eroticism?" O'Keeffe looked at him sharply. "Dirty ideas?" Parker nodded. "That's something people themselves put into my paintings. They've found things in my flowers and leaves, my skulls, even my mountains—things that never entered my mind."

"Folks say that's what you're famous for."

"What do *you* see in there, Parker Ray?"

Parker swallowed hard. "Lots of things. Different things. The more I look at it, the more I can find."

"So which, of all those ideas you are getting, did *I* have when I painted it?"

Parker shrugged.

"I could be thinking one thing and you could pick a whole other meaning, right? Art *makes* you think. It doesn't tell you *what* to think."

Parker nodded slowly, and said, "I've been doing a passel of thinking."

"Besides," O'Keeffe went on, "the things people say about my work always astonish me. Sexual imagery …" She shook her head. "It wouldn't occur to me."

Parker let out his breath.

"Well, that's that," O'Keeffe said, her voice businesslike again. "You shot the whole roll of film at dawn?"

"You bet," Parker said. He laughed. "Then I went back to sleep under the juniper for hours and hours."

O'Keeffe chuckled. "People don't know how exhausting it is to focus on a vision, do they?" Parker thought of O'Keeffe "just look-ing" at things. Or, if Clara was right, going into her trance.

"I was just sleepy," he explained.

"Well, I didn't get a nap today, so I am ready to turn in. You sharp enough to start developing the negatives now?"

Parker nodded. He wanted to stay up—to look at the new paint-ing through his own eyes again. Mostly he wanted to forget every-thing Clyde had said.

A scratching sound brought Parker and O'Keeffe to the door after breakfast the next morning. "Clara!" she said. "Did you bring my pot this time?"

"Good morning, Clara," Parker murmured. She flashed him a quick smile.

"May I come in?" she asked.

"Yes, yes," O'Keeffe said. They both followed her to the table where, Parker noticed, Clara did not even glance at the new painting. She carefully set a large basket on the table and lifted a pot out of the fabric wrappings inside. "Beautiful," O'Keeffe breathed.

The pot was round and smooth with a narrow mouth. The shape

was graceful, but the patterns painted on it in red, black, and white were dizzyingly complex. "You did this?" Parker asked.

"I am still learning," Clara said.

"She is a genius," O'Keeffe corrected.

"I do what Mother Clay allows," Clara said, ducking her head.

Parker fought a smile. This was a nice-looking pot, but Clara was just a little Indian kid, smart, but superstitious as all the rest. She was no genius.

"Parker," O'Keeffe said, "Clara found the clay as a rock, ground it fine, soaked it, formed it into a long, round snake and coiled it up into this shape, and smoothed it with her hands." Parker looked at Clara. The girl nodded. "Once it dried in the sun," O'Keeffe went on, "she baked it in a wood-fired oven and then polished it with a river stone until the surface was smooth enough to paint."

Parker stared at the pot. "That had to take days!" he said. "Where did you get your paints?"

"For the white, I ground white stone to powder, then mixed it with water. The red comes from red stone the same way."

"How did you get this black?" Parker picked up the pot carefully. He thought of the shadows in the cliff at dawn. None of them was as deep or as rich looking as the painted patterns traced across this pottery.

"Wild spinach," Clara said. "I pick it, make a tea of it, then boil that down to a thick, dark syrup."

"It's not black?" He stared at the pattern. The more he looked, the more brown tones he saw to the color. The herbal paint looked velvet soft on the pottery, not shiny like O'Keeffe's oils.

He glanced at the ram's skull painting. Its white wasn't really

white, he thought, just like the black in his hands wasn't black at
all, but a dark velvety brown. Nothing was as it seemed in art. Parker
shook his head. It was all a mirage.

The weight of the pottery in his hands made him remember
Clara. He looked at her face a moment and thought about all the
steps that she had gone through to make this one pot. He set it down
carefully in the center of the table and said, "I suppose you make
your own brushes, too?"

Clara nodded. "From yucca leaves."

Over at O'Keeffe's work area, jugs full of brushes sat ready. More
had arrived in the package from New York. A few tubes of colorful paint lay scattered about the table, but dozens, he knew, lay in
tidy boxes under the counter and in the Model A. His eyes met
O'Keeffe's, and he saw her respect. "Clara . . . ," Parker said, staring
again at the pot. He could not go on.

"It's not as if I discovered all this myself," Clara said. "My mother could do it, and her mother before her. Before that, it was an aunt.
Artists pass on their gifts. My mama gave me a handful of clay to play
with before I could walk."

"But you learned all this . . ." Parker suddenly wished his mother
had passed on something to him before she died.

"I brought a bowl for you, too," Clara said quietly, "if you will
have it."

"No," he began, but Clara was already unwrapping another piece
of pottery from within the basket. Soon Parker held a new bowl in
his hands, heavy and perfectly shaped. He could only think of the
hours Clara must have spent making it. He tipped it up to look at

the outside. The pattern was simple but regular, a series of stripes and budding leaves in white against black. The rich red covered the base of the bowl. A thin black stripe followed the top edge nearly all the way around.

"That line shows my life," Clara said. "I must leave an opening in it, or my life would close like the circle." Her voice was so serious that Parker knew she believed it.

He held the bowl in his cupped hands and looked inside. "The deer," he whispered. "Soi'ngwa."

"You know of the rain bringer?"

"Your brother told me. I looked down on a sleeping deer yesterday." He stared into the bowl. "He had antlers like this, and his eyes went this wide when they saw me."

"You wish so for rain, Parker, you see spirits."

"No, what I saw yesterday was just a deer," Parker said. He thought of the ram soaring above him. "I know the difference."

"Do you?" Clara asked.

"I have done paintings of a deer's skull over and over," O'Keeffe said, "but I have yet to catch its spirit." Her eyes had a faraway look to them. "Now I think I know a way that might work. . . ."

Parker laughed. "I feel another painting coming on."

"Hush," Clara said softly. She silently folded the fabrics back into the basket.

"How much do we owe you?" O'Keeffe asked, blinking. Clara named a price but refused to charge anything for Parker's bowl. "I only hope it brings what you yearn for," she said.

Parker laughed. "Rain. That would make everything better."

CHAPTER THIRTEEN

Rain

"Clara?" O'Keeffe said. "Have you ever tried painting on paper instead of on pottery?" Parker watched her pull a large pad of drawing paper from under the table.

Clara smiled and shook her head. "I serve Mother Clay," she said.

"What if you could earn money that way, too?" O'Keeffe moved a mug full of pencils to the table. "Tourists would buy paintings by a Pueblo girl. Even drawings."

"My family has always been potters," Clara said. "We are known for this."

"Do you have some time this afternoon?" O'Keeffe asked. "Parker has to wash my brushes. I have to touch up a painting." She gestured at the art supplies she'd laid out. "You could play here." Parker cringed.

"Play is for children," Clara said. "I must bring back money for the pots I have brought to sell at Ghost Ranch."

O'Keeffe glanced at the basket. "I will buy them all, now," she said triumphantly. "And I may well buy a drawing or two, as well."

Clara looked at her for a few breaths, then said, "What shall I draw?"

Parker grabbed the brushes and rags and stormed out of the casita rather than watch O'Keeffe push Clara around, too. He sat on the shady part of the bench and began wiping the paint and turpentine from the bristles. Their sharp stink matched his mood. So did a sky full of dark, towering clouds. It won't rain, he told himself. He knew the pattern. The day would heat up, and those clouds would build higher. Thunder would be rumbling by midafternoon. Lightning would flash over the mountains and rain would pour from the sky— but never make it to earth.

He sighed and carried the brushes indoors to wash. Clara was struggling to draw a deer on the paper as she had in the bottom of his bowl. She looked up at him and shrugged. "I need the roundness of clay to help me see the shape to draw."

Parker moved to the sink and started to work soap into the bristles of brush after brush. "Why did you agree to do this?"

"For money," she said. "My family needs it."

Parker looked into the sink. He turned on the faucet and stared at clean water splashing over his hands. A deep well and electric pumps made everything so easy. Running water in the house and flush toilets: Money made that possible, too. He coaxed the gluey soap on each brush into a lather, thinking, Money made everything possible, food and automobiles and even airplanes.

Parker squeezed the excess water from the brushes, wondering where he was going to get money. If, he thought, if I don't find Pa. For now, a job here and there was fine—but what if he wanted a house with electricity and flush toilets? What if he wanted three meals a day? He whipped the brushes at the sink, spraying their stored water in arcs into the basin. He had no land. He had no money. He had no schooling. With each thought he shook another brush dry. Worst of all, he told himself, he had no idea how he would ever get money.

"Parker! Where is your mind?" O'Keeffe said. He looked up. Droplets of water clung to the window over the sink and lay trembling all along the counter and the walls beyond.

"Aw, shucks," he said.

"It looks like it has rained in here," Clara said with a smile.

"It seems like it might storm outdoors, too," O'Keeffe said. "Look out the window."

The sun was behind a high dark cloud, and a nervous wind whipped branches in the courtyard. "It will never reach the ground," Parker muttered as he dropped the brushes, handle first, into a dry mug and headed out the door.

"Whoa!" he said, stepping away from the casita. The sky boiled above the little house. Long ago, he remembered dimly, a sky like this had dropped a tornado on a neighbor's land back in Texas. He raised his arms out to his sides to feel the wind.

"I love storms!" O'Keeffe cried as she hurried out of the casita, holding her hat to her head. Her face was flushed with color, and her eyes sparkled. "It might truly rain this time! What do you think, Parker?"

"I haven't seen rain in so long I've forgotten what it looks like."

"Here!" O'Keeffe said. "Come here!"

Parker hurried to join her as she crouched, peering at a flat rock.

A wet spot the size of a dime stained the sandstone. "That, Parker," she pronounced, "is a raindrop."

As they huddled over it, the damp spot shrank and faded. Soon the wind blew it dry.

"What are you looking at?" Clara said, joining them to stare at the dry rock.

"Rain," O'Keeffe said solemnly. Parker chuckled. A big drop splashed on his cheekbone and his head jerked back. Off balance, he fell to his seat. He wiped his eye as another drop hit his chin. Parker opened his mouth to the sky and waited.

Above him, the clouds thickened and shifted, rumbling ominously, but no more drops fell. "Well, that was exciting." Parker shook his head and looked about at the yard around the casita. A few damp spots speckled the adobe walls. The tidy line of little stones along the footpath showed some water marks. Most of O'Keeffe's collection of smooth, round desert stones were spotted, but all traces of water were fast evaporating. The plants were as wilted as ever.

"Back to work," O'Keeffe said with a sigh, but Clara was still looking up at the mesa.

"Taste it," she said. "Feel it along your skin. The rain spirit has heard your prayers, Parker."

"Oh, yes, powerful Soi'ngwa," he teased. "Wasn't that a great storm?"

"Open your eyes," she said. Parker followed her gaze. A curtain of gray swept along the top of the mesa. Far above it, a clap of thunder boomed. Lightning zigzagged to the mesa's cap rock, and the rain headed their way. One moment the cliff was in the clear; the next, it

was behind the wall of rain. It dropped from the cloud in a solid
sheet, shimmering and hissing as it fell. "Yee-haw!" Parker shrieked,
but a rumble of thunder drowned his cry. He wanted to run right
into the water. He wanted to run for cover. There was no time to
decide as the rain swept toward them.

"Holy cow!" he shouted as the first drops spattered against his
head, then, "Hey, it's cold!"

He looked at O'Keeffe. She was twirling, arms outstretched in the
rain. Clara was standing, head down, mumbling something. Then she
raised her head, looked at him, and smiled. Her black eyelashes were
full of raindrops, her skin slick with water.

"Rain! Rain! Rain!" Parker yelled. He spread his arms and raced
across the yard, flying through the storm, soaked to his skin with cool,
fresh water. Puddles splashed under his feet and raindrops the size of
grapes bounced against his shoulders. O'Keeffe was still doing her
crazy dance and laughing at him. Clara raised her hands to the sky.

Parker splashed his wet face with handfuls of water from a puddle. Now when he held his mouth open to the sky, he could taste—
and swallow—rain. The water was so cold it stung—and then it
did sting. "Hail?" He had forgotten all about that part of a storm.
"Take cover!"

There was a deafening crash of thunder as they all raced to the
overhang. Standing, backs pressed against the warm adobe, they
laughed as hailstones hit the ground, bounced back up, and rolled to
puddles. Parker struggled to remember the word for that. "Icebergs!"
he yelled, his voice barely louder than the roaring sound of ice balls
hitting their world.

O'Keeffe squatted down so she could reach a handful of ice without leaning out to get her head wet. She tossed the ice at Parker, though Clara got sprayed, too. Parker stepped out into the storm to gather a double handful and heave it back at her.

Soon all three were in on the battle, panting and shouting, squealing with surprise or yelling challenges across the yard. Parker flailed with his arms for balance as his feet slipped on the icy hailstones and slid on the mud. "Enough!" O'Keeffe finally cried.

The hail had stopped. Now rain pelted the ground in waves punctuated by the claps of thunder. Parker could just imagine the earth changing as it absorbed all this water. It had to be softening around him into the velvety soil he remembered as a child in the fields. He pulled off his boots and set them on the bench so he could feel the squishy mud between his toes.

Clara was walking down the path to the casita. She held her skirts up almost to her knees to keep them out of the runoff water rushing downhill. Parker laughed. Every bit of her was already soaked. He splashed over to join her in the flow. "Rio O'Keeffe!" Parker yelled to the artist. He had to shout three times before she finally heard him over the drumming rain, rushing water, and wild rumblings from the clouds above.

O'Keeffe pointed to the roof, where water gushed from the drainpipes in unending waterfalls. Parker grinned and nodded back at her, though he had no idea what she meant.

His bare feet could feel sand and stones rushing past in the dirty water that slid downhill. He squinted up toward the mesa but couldn't see where it all was coming from. When he looked around him, the entire slope was covered with muddy water, shifting and moving, racing downhill toward the driveway. He felt something brush his leg and jumped, then looked. It was a rattlesnake, swimming downstream, fighting to keep its head above water.

"Snake!" Parker yelled, and pointed. Through the rain he watched Clara follow O'Keeffe toward the house. Parker splashed his way downstream instead, while the rain pelted his head. The water was over his ankles now, bubbling and roaring along. In one eddy, a dead kangaroo rat floated in endless circles. Other water swung around a corner of the casita and joined a huge chaotic pond there stretching the length of the parking area. O'Keeffe's car sat in water midway up its doors. Parker remembered the artist comfortably lying under the car and quickly figured the pool to be a yard deep—and still the rain poured down.

Parker fought his way back uphill through the current until something soft squashed under his foot. A snake? Another rat? Parker jumped back, and the water shifted the sand beneath him. He lost his balance and fell, slipping and flailing into the floodwaters. He tumbled over and gagged. Sandy water filled his nose and the back of his throat. Parker rolled to all fours, raised his head, and gasped the rain-filled air. By crawling and keeping close to the house, he managed to work his way uphill.

He stopped by the corner of the casita. The adobe wall was washing away. "O'Keeffe!" he screamed. The mud covering was gone, and the bricks beneath were exposed. The waterborne sand and stones that had stung at his calves and filled his mouth were eating away at the casita itself. "O'Keeffe!" he screamed again.

"Up!" her voice yelled back. "Look up!" Parker put his hand up to protect his eyes from the furious rainfall and tried to find O'Keeffe against the thundercloud. "Come up!" she cried from above, though he still could not see her. He looked down. The water was rising against his legs and surging on downhill. Was the casita flooded?

Parker fought his way upstream and gasped to see the water lapping inches deep against the door. He turned the handle and leaped inside, rushing to grab O'Keeffe's paintings from the corner before the water could reach them. He stacked them on top of the table and glanced around the room. Muddy water dripped right through the ceiling onto the counter, puddled there, and drained off, splashing onto the flooded floor. Parker wondered how deep it was going to get. His breathing felt as wild and fast as the storm itself. Parker took a long slow breath and forced himself to think. The paintings and the people. Nothing else had to be saved. Just the paintings and the people. Just himself.

Parker pushed the door open against the water, then let the flood slam it behind him. He slogged against the current and finally turned to the side of the house. "Oh, no!" he cried. The ladder was gone. "O'Keeffe!"

The ladder slid down through the rain from above. Parker grabbed it and set the bottom into the water. The current tried to sweep it from his grasp, but he held on. He began climbing, hoping his weight would stabilize the ladder's feet.

Near to the top, he paused in awe. To each side of him, water hurled out of the gutters, it pounded on his head, and it roared in a flood below. He felt hands grasping at his arms and pulled himself up over the edge of the roof. Water stood inches deep on the roof, too, though it gurgled down through each gutter. He glanced toward the area of the kitchen and saw an eddy where the water churned a channel down through the layers of mud and sticks, between the rafters, through the ceiling, and into the casita.

A swath of lightning hit the cottonwood by the casita. Thunder cracked the sky open and reverberated through Parker's head as the bark exploded off the tree. He blinked, trying to see through the blue burn flashes in his eyes. Was the tree going to fall on them, too?

It didn't, though he had every muscle tightened and ready. The rain felt cold now as he huddled next to Clara and O'Keeffe, hoping that the adobe would not give way below them. O'Keeffe wrapped her wet, bony arm around his shoulders, and Parker let himself lean into her warmth.

"This could be bad," O'Keeffe said.

Parker looked around the casita. "I wanted it to rain," he said, his voice breaking.

"And it did. Look, it is tapering off." The three of them sat against the corner while the rain slowed to a drizzle and the thunder died away. They didn't move until the sun peeked out below the cloud.

Clara pointed silently to a rainbow arcing in the sky.

Parker wiped his wet face with his wet hand and clambered to his knees in the muddy adobe. "Thank God it's over," he said. Then he looked over the edge of the roof.

The ladder was gone, and below them, a flash flood raged past.

CHAPTER FOURTEEN

Ruin

"It's just as well," O'Keeffe said when Parker told her the ladder was gone. "We shouldn't move until the water goes down some."

Parker stared at the cottonwood tree where lightning had hit. In a great spiral gash from top to bottom of its trunk, pale wood steamed naked in the sunlight. Shreds and sheets of charred bark dangled around the edges of the scar. Branches hung broken and stripped. Leaves littered the roof nearby and smoke curled upward from chunks of bark hurled from the exploding tree. Parker thought to kick them off, but remembered he had left his boots below. In the water.

He looked down again. A foreign landscape lay below him. Where O'Keeffe had insisted on tidiness, the yard was chaos. Plants torn from her garden lay strewn about, broken. Muddy water surged past in new channels it had carved down the slope. Everywhere, sticks and tumbleweeds, cactus and torn leaves lay scattered about or clogging the new streams. Somehow, the sun shown warmly over all, as if nothing had happened.

Parker closed his eyes and felt the sun on his face. His shirt was drying on his back, and his jeans pulled tight against his knees. His stomach told him dinner was overdue. That, at least, felt normal. He kept his eyes closed. O'Keeffe's voice murmured to Clara nearby. The wind was soft again, and some bird chirped in a nearby tree. Parker could almost believe nothing had happened, but he could not ignore the sounds of water, dripping and gurgling and eating away at the very house he lived in.

Rain was not supposed to be this way. This was wrong, his mind insisted; so wrong. Parker felt a hand on his arm. He opened his eyes to see Clara looking at him. His stomach clenched at the look of sympathy in her small face. "Let go of me," he said, jumping to his feet. "It's all your fault, you and your rain bringer."

"Parker." O'Keeffe's voice held a caution.

"Can't you see?" he flung at her. "It's ruined. All of it." He swung his arm wide to show her the devastation around the casita. A branch fell from the cottonwood, landing with a splashing thump below. "It's hopeless now."

"But . . ." Clara's soft voice infuriated Parker.

"No!" he heard himself shout. "I have to go down there. I have to see how bad it is." Clara and O'Keeffe were nattering like birds in the distance as he decided to jump for the top of the garden wall. It didn't look too slippery. Parker swung his legs over the edge of the roof, leaned down, and grabbed the end of a rafter. The birds shrieked as he dropped to hang from his hands, swinging. Parker stretched his bare toes, but they did not quite reach the wall. He rocked to the side and let go, feeling one heel smash into the adobe below. He fell forward and landed in the water.

"Parker!" O'Keeffe yelled from above.

"I'm fine," he called back angrily, and struggled to his feet. He limped away, feeling the twist and jolt of his landing along the length of his back. "I'm getting the ladder."

He looked around under the overhang. Flowers trailed in the mud. Debris had caught against this side of the casita, sticks and leaves, mostly, and a dead lizard. Parker waded around the building, looking for damage. The flow of water was easing now, but it had carved through the bricks on the corner. Parker knelt in the mud and leaned down, groaned at a twinge in his back. He peered into the gaping hole. The flood had not made it through the thick wall.

The world glistened raw and brown everywhere. The dirt had turned to mud, the water was mud filled, and the low plants were mud caked. Brown water coursed through new-carved channels splitting the paths and making islands of the yard. Next to the battered body of a rat, a tortoise lay on its back, thrashing its legs helplessly.

"I know how you feel," Parker mumbled, flipping the animal back onto its feet.

In the distance, the mountains glowered under the dark thundercloud, but the casita sparkled in insanely bright sunshine. Parker glared at a butterfly that dared to flutter across the strange moonscape.

"Parker?" O'Keeffe's voice called from above. He stood and saw the ladder in a drift of shredded cottonwood bark and limbs. The entire soggy mess had lodged against the base of the tree. He heaved the wreckage out of the way, relishing the action, even if it meant pain in his back. He grabbed the ladder, hauled it over to the casita, and settled it against the wall.

"Ready," he yelled. "Ladder's here." When Parker stepped back to see if Clara or O'Keeffe was going to climb down, his heel landed on something sharp under the water. "Drat!" he cursed, hopping on his good foot. He stepped carefully toward the doorway, looking for his boots.

One of them lay next to the bench on its side in a puddle. He held it up to pour out its contents. The water flowed into a nearby channel. Parker limped down the muddy trail left by the current, cursing quietly under his breath. It had all been a lie, he thought. Rain hadn't made anything better at all. His feet squished on through the mud. How many footsteps had he walked, he wondered, hoping to get away from the drought and the dust and the death? If rain won't fix things—he shook his head slowly at the thought—nothing will.

He stopped to stare at a baby jackrabbit lying on its side, its fur clogged with mud. It wasn't moving. In a smeary way, it seemed to be sleeping there. Parker considered lying down beside it. He wondered how it would feel to let himself be so limp.

"You looking for this?" O'Keeffe asked at his side. Silently, Parker took his other boot from her. He sat down in the mud next to the dead animal and slowly pulled his wet boots over his muddy feet. "I painted a dead rabbit once, when I was about your age," O'Keeffe said. "Got me a scholarship. It was the first time anybody believed I had a future as an artist. Even me."

A future. O'Keeffe's words dripped through Parker's mind. *A future?* He fought to make sense of the words as he watched a fly land on the rabbit's ear. The fly crawled down inside, then stopped to wipe its face with its front feet. *A future.*

"Come inside," O'Keeffe said calmly. Parker took her hand. She gave him a surprisingly strong heave to help him to his feet, then walked with him to the casita. Water stood in a muddy puddle on the kitchen counter, though the dripping from the ceiling had stopped. The floors were slick and wet.

"Clara said she knew a way out over the mesa," O'Keeffe said, pouring him some carrot juice. "She left to find her family's camp. Santo Domingo Pueblo is on the Rio Grande, so she's had plenty of practice with storm flooding. You weren't serious when you said it was her fault, were you?"

Parker didn't bother trying to remember what he had said. It did not matter. Nothing did now. The rain had come, and nothing had changed. He gazed at the cup of carrot juice in his hand and wondered why it was there.

"It's a lucky thing you came in," O'Keeffe said. Parker looked at her, mildly surprised by what she was saying. She held up a painting and eyed its edges, then flipped it over and checked the back. "No water damage. That was quick thinking. Water can ruin a painting, or a photogr— Oh, my." She put her hands to her mouth and fled the room.

Parker limped after her into her bedroom. O'Keeffe was on her knees on the muddy floor, pulling out the bottom drawers of her night table. She grabbed a handful of black-and-white photographs and threw them onto the bed, fanning them out wide. "Thank heavens," she said, her hands moving rapidly, separating the prints and wiping the backs of some of them against the white bedspread. Parker stared.

There were somber city views and perfect fruits in bowls, gaunt old men, and foreign-looking women against a beach. There were huge factories, clouds, a naked woman, slender and strong looking.

Parker wanted to look away, but he had to stare at the body, so beautiful and unreal in her silvery gray skin. His own body respond-ed as he looked at her arms and breasts lifting up into the light, or her body twisted upward as if dancing for joy. Other pictures showed her backside, round as a piece of fruit, or the front of her standing proud and fearless before the camera. Parker stared until he saw one of the pictures that included the woman's head. He closed his eyes. It was O'Keeffe.

"Aren't they beautiful?" O'Keeffe asked. "He is a genius."

"Who?" Parker forced himself to ask.

"Why, Alfred," O'Keeffe said. "My husband. Alfred Stieglitz. He exhibits his photographs in New York City."

"*Those photographs?*" Parker stared at the wall and tried to con-trol the trembling in his muscles.

O'Keeffe laughed in delight. "Yes," she said. "*Those.* At first it bothered me, but Alfred has made art of my plain old body. Now I rather like it, don't you?"

Parker's face burned with embarrassment.

"Haven't you had pictures of yourself that you enjoy looking at?" she asked. Parker's hand flew up to his shirt pocket. The fabric was still soaking wet and he had to pry the flap open before he could reach inside. He groaned in horror as his fingers touched the slimy surface of his family's photograph. "Stop!" O'Keeffe said. "Take off your shirt." Parker felt his face flame again. "No, silly," she scolded briskly. "I can get the picture out of there. And maybe Alfred can fix any damage for you."

"Why would he do that?" Parker asked.

"He is an artist," O'Keeffe said. She took his shirt out into the kitchen. "Wait there," she called back to him. Parker stood in his wet boots and jeans, shivering. O'Keeffe was everywhere, and naked. He stared. She wasn't like the show-hall dancers he'd snuck in to see at a carnival this summer. O'Keeffe's body was almost gaunt, but very strong.

Parker tried to forget he knew whose body he was looking at. That did not work. He tried to shift his mind as he had when he saw the cliff as if it weren't in colors. Only now he was trying to look at a naked body as if it wasn't naked. As if he didn't know the woman. As if she wasn't next door, rattling things around in the kitchen, calm as could be. His body would not let him forget.

He made himself walk into the kitchen. Parker was relieved to see O'Keeffe facing out the window. "Um," he began, "some time could I look at those other pictures? The ones that"—he swallowed hard—"aren't . . . you."

"Of course," O'Keeffe said. "But we have a lot of work to do around here first." She laid his family photograph on the windowsill and Parker winced.

"I wish Pa had gotten somebody really good to take our pictures. Somebody like your husband."

"Wishing never got anybody anything," O'Keeffe said flatly. Parker thought about wishing for rain. Where had it gotten him? He sighed.

"Sighing isn't worth much, either," O'Keeffe snapped. "Don't wallow in your troubles. Dance." She struck a pose, twisting upward and looked into his eyes expectantly. For a moment, Parker wondered what she was doing. Then he blushed.

"That's better!" She swatted him with the dishtowel and chuckled.

CHAPTER FIFTEEN

Green

"For someone who always had a line ready"—O'Keeffe leaned on her broom—"you've been mighty quiet lately."

"Not much to say, I guess." Parker hurled a shovel of sand into the last gully across the path and stamped it down.

"Cabin fever?" O'Keeffe asked. "Feels like weeks since I've gotten out on my rounds."

"It hasn't quite been a week. Clyde came by and said the roads are almost ready for auto traffic again."

"That sweet young man came by?" When Parker didn't answer, she snapped, "That was a joke, Parker." She stepped into the casita.

Parker stretched his back carefully. His bruised heel was back to normal, but his back would take more time. He searched the sky for rainclouds, then caught himself. "Don't want rain," he reminded himself, then wondered what he *did* want. Parker dumped another shovelful into the ditch and let himself go again in the simple muscle motion.

A week of wiping and shoveling, raking and mopping and hauling brush, had given him plenty of mindless hours. Parker had tied lines across the sunny yard and carted out soaking clothes and bedding, rugs and cushions to dry. He'd fallen asleep as soon as he'd hit the bed each night, too, so there was little space for thinking. Parker had liked it that way. No starry roof nights with O'Keeffe, either. She'd even been too busy to paint.

O'Keeffe had pulled her weight, putting the casita back to livable order even though Merita scolded her. Parker liked that, when he stopped to think about it. He grabbed a rake and threw himself into smoothing sand over the flood damage.

"Time we got some fresh air." O'Keeffe burst out of the casita door, her arms full. "You and I have *got* to get out into the desert again." She thrust a sloshing canteen at him, his hat, a lunch pail and backpack, and a camera, too. Parker had to drop the rake to grab it all. "You head out east. I'll go west. I'll see you here for supper." She paused for a breath. "After you meet some of the guests tonight, we'll look at Alfred's pictures together."

Parker opened his mouth to protest.

"Oh, not *those* pictures, I promise you," O'Keeffe said. "Now scoot. Make tracks. Vamoose." She turned on her heel and headed back to the house. "Don't forget supper tonight with the paying guests," she called back to him. "Be back in time to clean yourself up some."

"Yes, ma'am," he said, then waited a heartbeat for her response.

"That's O'Keeffe to you!" she yelled, and laughed gaily. Parker found himself grinning as he began stuffing all the bundles into his pack.

🌿🌿🌿

Parker had to leap a deep gully to get onto the main road. He landed in a spray of dust and looked up and down the road. It was so
quiet that it seemed more like a ghost road than a main street.
Goose bumps prickled along Parker's arms. They did that a lot here,
he thought. There was something about this part of New Mexico,
or maybe about the Pueblo Indians or the desert air, that didn't
show distances; but the place felt haunted, even without Ghost
Ranches and magical spirit deer.

He looked closer at the road. There were no tire tracks along
this stretch, but hoofprints dimpled its surface and dung beetles
swarmed over fresh horse droppings. Every beetle had the same
markings and sun glints on their backs, and they all were so
intent on their work that the action was a lovely pattern—even on
horse turds.

Parker wondered about taking a photograph of it all and told
himself it couldn't be any worse than pictures of naked women.

He knelt on the road and raised the camera. Through the viewfinder, the jumble of black and orange beetles looked like a kaleido-
scope vision. He snapped a shot. A flicker of motion caught his eye
and he stared at a beetle pushing a dung ball along. Parker lay on
his side to focus on the little animal. He grinned at the picture that he
himself would make and clicked the shutter.

Parker glanced down the empty road and decided that the
sound of hoofbeats or boot heels would let him know in plenty of
time that someone was coming. A breeze blew any stink away. Parker
relaxed. Overhead, ravens called. A lizard stalked the beetles but

flicked away when it realized a big human was lying there. Parker felt his back muscles slowly release as the sun baked through his shirt and the skin beneath.

A cool shadow fell on his back. Parker twisted to see who was there, then winced. "Do not move," Clara said.

"What are you doing here?" Parker demanded. He looked at her bare feet, silent in the dust of the road.

"I've come to be sure O'Keeffe is well after the storm." Clara ducked her head. "Also you. And I wanted to ask for more paper."

She squatted comfortably next to him and stared at the beetles. "They have dignity," she said.

Parker sat up. They laughed as a beetle fell over and its dung ball rolled away. "Maybe, but sometimes they just look foolish," Parker said. The beetle scurried to catch its runaway prize and laboriously rolled it back where it wanted it. As the beetle scratched a hole beneath its trophy, Parker thought about what O'Keeffe had said. "Clara," he admitted, "I was foolish, too, after the rain." She shook her head, but he went on. "It wasn't your fault."

"It wasn't yours, either, Parker," she said quietly. "For all your longing, you were making your way before the storm. You have spirit enough now to follow any path." He felt the last of the tension flow from his shoulders. They watched the beetles for a few moments in silence.

Parker glanced at O'Keeffe's camera. "May I take your picture?" he asked Clara.

She raised her hands to pat her hair into place. "No," he said quickly. "I'd like to catch the spirit of you, quiet here by the roadside." He flipped the viewfinder open and she grinned broadly at the camera. "No, just look at the beetles for a moment."

Clara leaned forward, and Parker noticed her dark lashes falling onto her cheekbones as her eyes lowered. Her face softened. As she watched the intense action on the road, Clara's lips parted with concentration. Parker felt his face flush as if he were looking at something very private through the viewfinder. He *was* seeing something very lovely. He watched as tiny changes in Clara's face reflected her thoughts about the little beetles with all their "dignity." *Snap!* The shutter's sound made them both jump.

Clara stood up, and Parker pushed himself to his feet. "Thank you," they both said at once, and laughed. "I must go to O'Keeffe," Clara said.

"Oh, she is out rambling, too, to the west," Parker said. "I'll let her know you were asking for her when I see her tonight."

"Good," Clara said. "The season is passing."

Parker shifted from foot to foot, not wanting to say good-bye. "Perhaps I'll see William this afternoon," he said.

"I hope you do," Clara smiled. "I'm sure we'll meet again, too." She turned and walked silently down the road. Parker decided to hike toward the melting mountain. William often grazed his sheep near there.

Every step of the trip felt different. The ditches were deeper, and rain had scoured them clean. New channels crisscrossed the flats. Parker saw a seashell half buried in the side of a new gully. He climbed down to take a picture of the dark shell in its pale bed. When he pried the shell out, three more fell from the crumbling rock. Parker stared at them in his hand. They were stone, not shell. He put them into his pack and moved on.

Each little cactus had a pale green bud at its tip. The dried tussocks of grass had new sprouts at their bases, too. Stalks whipped clean by wind and rain stood free of dead leaves and dust, so every plant looked new. Even the juniper at the base of the cliff looked fresh.

Parker got his camera ready. Things had changed. There, where a torrent had washed downward, a new streak of white glazed the cliff. Dark gray boulders had loosened from the top and rolled downhill. Loose tan dust had been rinsed off below the layer of yellow rock, changing everything below. It was a new cliff, he thought, snapping picture after picture.

He sat down under the juniper and ate cold tortillas wrapped around cheese and refried beans until the waist of his jeans bit into his skin. Parker ran his thumbs along inside his belt and laughed. He surely had been eating well! He drank some water and stared at the top of the cliff. Perhaps he could see William from there, he thought.

There was no shepherd in sight when he reached the cap rock. Instead, the Sangre de Cristo Mountains spread along the horizon, tall and crisp in the clean air. Parker took a deep breath and sat down on the ledge. Birds had left white splatters there since the rain, and fluffs of down were caught in the wiry grass growing in a crack. Parker imagined a golden eagle sitting where he was, looking out over the plain. He leaned back, and his hand brushed an old arrowhead. It was a tiny one, a bird point, delicately fluted along its edge but solid rock all the same. He photographed it in the grass tussock with the feathers. When he moved behind the grass and lay down to take a picture that included the mountains, too, he found he was out of film.

From that height, the desert plain looked different, and it took Parker a few moments to figure out why. It was the color. The desert was not quite the dead tans and grays he was used to seeing. There was the faintest hint of sage green now to every tuft of grass and a hint of apple green about the cactus. There seemed to be a pale shimmer of green over everything. Parker wondered if it were a mirage.

Looking toward the sun, he gulped. It was nearly sunset. O'Keeffe had insisted that he be back early to clean himself up. She had stressed that dinner was with the "dudes," not the ranch hands. He hurried down the back of the mountain and on toward Ghost Ranch.

"Develop the negatives tonight," O'Keeffe said. "You can do the prints tomorrow." Parker wanted to ask what the hurry was, but the whole evening had been a jumble. First, O'Keeffe had bought him new clothes for dinner. They fit, for a change. Then, the "dudes" at this dude ranch were not what he had expected at all. They dressed all fancy, their table manners would have made even Mama happy, and they ate off pretty plates while a ranch hand played guitar. But these weren't boring high society types. They were writers and scientists. They had interesting stories, and they were interested in *him*, too.

A dinosaur scientist made Parker promise to bring him the fossil shells tomorrow. Some lady asked about his mother's cough. She claimed she was a doctor. One of the writers wanted to hear details of how a dust storm felt. Arthur Pack told such a wonderful story of flying that Parker ached to be in the air.

And O'Keeffe was different at supper. She joked and teased until the entire table was roaring with laughter. As soon as they got back to the casita, though, she dropped into a chair, threw off her shoes, and said "God, I hate the social scene." Then she demanded, "Do you remember everybody's names?"

She insisted that he recall details about everyone and filled him in where he hadn't paid attention. There was the city woman who loved horses. One banker, a Mr. Bishop, had a cactus garden in his green-house in New York City. "Oh, his wife is the one with all the jewel-ry, right?" Parker said. O'Keeffe reminded him about the newlyweds who had trouble looking at anyone but each other. Parker wanted to ask what it mattered. He wanted to sit somewhere where his back wouldn't hurt so. He wanted to go to sleep, but O'Keeffe quizzed him again on everyone's names before she pulled out a box of photographs.

True to her word, she had weeded out all the pictures of herself. What was left were mostly landscapes, cityscapes, and portraits. One by one she went over the details of their composition and lighting, tricks her husband had used in each shot, and what she would have done differently. It was interesting, but Parker was yawning long before she was done.

Then O'Keeffe said, "Develop the negatives tonight." While he got the chemical baths ready, she prepared to go up onto the newly repaired roof to sleep. "If I fall through, just dust me off," she told him, "and throw a blanket over me wherever I lie." He was too tired to smile.

Parker left the negatives hanging over the sink when he went to bed.

CHAPTER SIXTEEN

About Face

"What . . .?" Parker awoke to the sound of Arthur Pack's plane taking off. He blinked and looked at the window in his tiny room. At the sight of bright sunlight, he threw off the covers. "O'Keeffe?" he called.

When there was no answer, Parker yawned and scratched himself. The artist would be long gone on her morning rounds by now. He yawned again, lay back on the mattress, and tried to remember when he had ever slept in so late.

At last his bladder would wait no longer, and Parker rolled out of bed and hurried toward the bathroom. "*Buenos dias.*" Merita stood by the sink. Parker glanced down at the holes and rips in his old underwear and blushed. Merita giggled and pointed toward the bathroom. Parker ran for cover.

When he was finished, Parker waited, hoping he would hear the door shut as the maid left. He flushed with anger, imagining Clyde's harsh laughter when his girlfriend told him about the scene. Finally she called, "You can come out now. I won't look." Parker stared at the ceiling, weighing his options, before he took a deep breath and dashed back to the bedroom. Merita took a good look at him this time—but she didn't laugh.

With his old jeans and shirt firmly buttoned and his boots and hat for extra height, Parker attempted what he hoped was a cool saunter back to the kitchen. Merita was busy wiping the table now, her gold cross swinging in the low neckline of her white blouse. "It was good to see you up, finally," Merita said. Parker froze. "I mean . . . not that," she colored. "Really, I didn't . . . I'm not that kind." She buried her face in her hands and turned away, hitting the jar of clean paintbrushes with her elbow.

O'Keeffe's tools crashed to the floor, scattering everywhere. Both Parker and Merita stooped to gather them. "You will think I'm clumsy," she apologized, her face inches from his.

"Not at all." Parker winked at her. "If you won't think I'm forward." Now she froze, and then they were both laughing. Teasing her, he thought, was easier with his clothes on. He grinned again. "There," he finally said, as the last brush plunked into the bottom of the jar. "All back to normal."

"*Gracias,*" Merita said, smiling. "*Gracias.*" Suddenly she looked startled. "Oh, no!" she said. "O'Keeffe left something for you at the main house. I was to say so as soon as you—" She stopped.

"I'll tell her it was my fault," he said. "I distracted you." They both laughed, and Parker walked out with a spring in his step.

"Good morning, Parker," a tall man said on the way to Arthur Pack's house. "Where's your camera?" Parker looked up in surprise. Any other day he would just have tipped his hat and walked past the "dude." He struggled to remember the man's name. Bishop. The cactus banker. "You really don't want to miss this," the man was saying. "The desert should start blooming today."

"Well, Mr. Bishop, sir." Parker nodded, thinking furiously. His camera? Had they discussed that at the table last night? "Thank you for reminding me," he chattered on. "You have a good day, now, you hear?"

"Oh, Parker," Phoebe Pack called out as he walked into the main house. "Here." She reached below the counter and handed him the old camera. "O'Keeffe said you might be needing this." She gazed out the window. "Promise me you'll tell me tonight if the desert is flowering yet. It's God's gift, for sure." She sighed. "I could take tomorrow off and wander."

Parker nodded his thanks and left.

The desert was blooming. Parker had only to walk the length of the driveway to see that. Yellow and red flowers speckled the wasteland, and the faint green had strengthened to a glow. He stopped by a cholla to look at its blossoms, strangely pretty against the wicked spines. Parker looked down at the camera in his hands. It was loaded with a fresh roll of film.

O'Keeffe meant for him to take *more* pictures? He'd finished an entire roll yesterday and left the negatives over the sink. Clara's picture was in that batch.

"Well, dang!" he cussed, wondering where they had gone. He tried to picture the kitchen this morning and could only see Merita's cross, swinging, low. Parker grinned, then thought of himself in his sorry underwear. He shook his head, then grinned again. He couldn't have looked too bad. Merita was still speaking with him. And those negatives were dry, anyway. They were probably piled safe in a corner somewhere.

He looked through the viewfinder at a blossom tucked between two tufts of spines. It was almost open, and the dark shadows in the branches set it off just right. Parker put his finger on the shutter but didn't push. Another few hours and that flower would peak. Parker decided he would come back before supper. The lighting would be better then, too.

He scanned the horizon. A thin dark figure stood hunched in the distance. Parker strode in that direction. As he got closer it resolved into O'Keeffe in her black jeans and shirt and her broad black hat. She was sketching on a big pad propped at her waist. Now and then, she would squat to pull something from a little suitcase and rise to work again.

He walked quietly up behind her. The box at her feet held squares of chalk, not paints. Blue and green dust streaked O'Keeffe's hands, but it looked as if she had almost finished her drawing. Parker held his breath and readied the camera. Through the viewfinder, O'Keeffe looked like part of the desert. Under the hat, her black hair twisted into a bun as tight as the flower buds she drew. The skin of her neck was as tan and weathered as any old cowhand's.

"Don't you dare, Parker Ray," she said. "Don't you even think of it."

"Why?" he asked.

"I thought I'd work up sketches of this as it opened," she answered. "The colors change, see?" She tipped the pad so he could look. He didn't.

"That's not what I meant," Parker said, adding quickly, "nice picture. But why can't I photograph you?"

"Only Alfred does."

"He does the pictures of you for magazine covers, too?"

"You know about that?" O'Keeffe sighed. "No, Parker, professional photographers have often snapped my photos." She took off her hat and wiped her forehead with a handkerchief. "Let's find some shade." They looked around at the flat stretch of desert and laughed together. "Well, we could sit down at least. Did you bring water?" Parker shook his head. "Oh, Parker," she scolded, and then settled to the ground, crossing her legs. There was a bit of spotty shade from the cholla bush she was drawing, and O'Keeffe had a small canteen tucked in her chalk box.

"Do you remember," she asked once he was settled, "how glad I was that you'd chased away those tourists with their cameras?" Parker nodded. "I don't want photographs of me out there that people could sell or use just for souvenirs. What if they were ugly pictures?"

"Of *you*?" Parker couldn't imagine her looking ugly.

"Oh, ho, Parker, you flatter me," O'Keeffe said. "But did you know some Indians don't want their pictures taken because they think it steals part of their spirit away?"

"And Alfred wouldn't steal your spirit?" Parker teased. He thought of the beautiful photographs of her spread on the bed.

"Oh, Alfred has done worse than that." O'Keeffe looked at the distant mountains. "He put up a display of my drawings in his studio before I even knew he had them." To Parker's startled gasp,

she answered, "I was young, and it got my career going." She seemed
to be thinking, so Parker stayed silent. "Then, in another exhibit,"
she said, "he used some of those photographs you saw of me, printed large. I didn't know about that one, either, until I walked into the
show and saw dozens of strangers looking at my body."

Parker cringed. "The scoundrel!"

"You are too sweet." O'Keeffe patted Parker's knee. "Alfred will
do anything for his art—or to help a young artist, for that matter.
Besides," she added to the far mountains, "he loves me."

She didn't have to say she loved him, too, Parker thought. It was
there in her voice. "I wish he could come here and see me where I am
happy." She laughed sharply. "He says the United States ends at the
Mississippi, so he just stays East, at his family place on Lake George
or in our apartment in New York City, while I come here, where I
feel at home. Where the magic is . . .

"Enough of this," she said, getting to her feet. She brushed off her
jeans and picked up the pad again. Parker put the canteen back into
her art box.

"I'll see you back at the casita?" he asked.

"Parker," she said. "You may take my photograph now."

She insisted he dress in his new clothes and come to dinner at the dining room again that night. A different group of guests sat at the table.
Parker tried to remember all the details about them, to be ready for
O'Keeffe's quiz. One loved sunsets. Another had brought all her
children along. A third couple talked about nothing but their church.

Merita came to the table and asked if anyone wanted wine.

"Champagne for the both of us," O'Keeffe said loudly, and winked at Merita. "It's a party."

Parker stared at the faces around the table. They all seemed to know what was happening. He wished he did. When the champagne came, O'Keeffe held her glass high and looked at him. "Well, Parker, you are a free man. You have served a month's time with me—and lived to tell the tale." The others laughed and clapped. Parker wanted to slide beneath the tablecloth.

"Wait," she said. "There's more." She nodded at Merita. "Drink some champagne," she commanded Parker. He remembered choking on whiskey in Clyde's car when he'd first arrived—was that only a month ago? Then he took a careful sip of champagne. Apple juice, he identified the taste, or grape juice, but soured and fizzy. He took another sip.

"Not so fast," she said, and, while others at the table chuckled, O'Keeffe handed him a box. Parker looked at her in surprise. "Open it."

Inside the box was a camera. It was like the one she had loaned him, but new, brand new. Parker's mind raced, trying to imagine the cost of such a gift. "I can't take this." He shook his head. "I really can't."

"Nonsense," O'Keeffe snapped.

"But what am I going to do with it? I live on the road."

"Well," the sunset lover said, "back home all the fancy restaurants and clubs have photographers who will take your picture." She paused and added meaningfully, "For a price."

"This isn't New York City," Parker said.

"But most of us *are* city people," the church lady said. "And we must have souvenirs to take home."

Parker thought of Clara's souvenir pots. "Would you trust me to take your picture?" he asked.

"Trust you?" Her husband laughed. "We'd *pay* you."

"So would I," Mr. Bishop called from the next table. "Can we arrange a sitting for tomorrow?" Parker blinked. Everyone seemed to be in on this.

He met O'Keeffe's eyes over the table. "I've heard tell," she said, "there's even a need for traveling photographers who can take decent shots." Parker swallowed. "There's film in the box," she said. "And, for now, you can pay me for the use of my chemicals and pans." She lifted her glass again. "Deal?"

Not knowing what else to do, Parker nodded, and took another swallow of champagne.

CHAPTER SEVENTEEN

Faces

"Mr. Bishop?" Parker found the man in his casita after breakfast the next morning. "I could take your picture now."

"Only if you can have the prints ready in a couple of days. We're leaving after the big Indian powwow this weekend. Bunch of us heading out together."

Parker thought fast. "No problem, sir. Not if I take the shots today."

"Well, well, m'boy," the banker said. "I surely do appreciate an enthusiastic young businessman." Parker had to think twice to realize that the man was talking about him. "Do you want me and the little woman to pose over there?" Mr. Bishop pointed to the adobe fireplace built into the corner of the casita.

"I'll just get my pearls. . . ," Mrs. Bishop said. She ducked into her bedroom.

"Well, no, sir," Parker said. "Actually, I saw a cactus flowering at the end of the driveway yesterday. I thought you might like a portrait with that."

"Oh, capital!" the banker said. "But what about Henny, here?" He gestured at his wife, now thoroughly bejeweled.

"You could leave the pearls here," Parker said. "You'd be just as happy with a string of mountains in the background, wouldn't you?"

She was.

Arthur Pack was happy, too, when Parker offered to pose him in the cockpit of his airplane. Parker remembered to bring the fossil shells when he took the scientist's picture. He put a sugar cube in his pocket so when it was the horsewoman's turn, he could snap the shutter as a horse lipped the treat off her palm. He watched each guest through his viewfinder until a look of pleasure came over his or her face; then he snapped the shutter, tried another pose and waited until the "dude" relaxed before exposing more film. Whenever he felt like hurrying, he remembered the one spiritless picture he had of his family.

"You've got to tell them all that I am busy developing," Parker said breathlessly when O'Keeffe came in off the desert. "I can't do dinner at the main house again tonight." He turned back to the sink.

"Oh, yes, you can," she said firmly, taking off her dusty hat. "You need these people now." She looked at the forest of negatives he had already strung up over the sink and smiled approvingly. "You did quote them the price I suggested?"

"Gosh sakes, yes," Parker said, "and not a one of them argued with me."

"Well, there isn't anyone else around to offer cheaper photographs.

Did you remember everything we talked about?" O'Keeffe demanded. "Lighting and angles and focus?"

"Probably not," Parker said, and sighed. Then he grinned. "But
then I am the only show in town."

"You'll learn those lessons the hard way, then," O'Keeffe snapped,
"when you see today's mistakes."

At the dinner table, the guests who'd had their pictures taken talked
about Parker's technique. "He showed me a new species of cactus!"
Mr. Bishop said. The horsewoman raved about the whiskery feel
of horse lips on her palm until someone made a rude comment.
When Arthur demanded that Phoebe pose in the cockpit, too, she
squealed in horror, and everyone laughed. Others introduced themselves, and soon Parker realized he would have to spend all night
printing photographs simply to have enough time to complete the
next day's new orders.

By dawn, he had completed the bulk of the lab work. By noon, he'd
taken pictures of the church couple against the most inspiring set of
rock pinnacles on the Ghost Ranch, a pair of little children sitting
astride a palomino pony, and an older woman amid the piles of
Pueblo Indian pottery she'd collected as souvenirs. When he told the
newlyweds to pose however they'd like, the new husband twined
himself around his bride. "Bet you won't take this shot!"

"Hold it right there!" Parker had said, blushing, and clicked the
shutter. He remembered how calm O'Keeffe was about her naked-
body photos and he suggested that the couple hold each other and

kiss as passionately as they wished before his lens. They would, he thought, be happy with the results.

By midafternoon, he was done. The processing took the rest of the day. By dinnertime, he had finished photographs to sell. He was very happy with some of them, and satisfied with most of the rest. As O'Keeffe had predicted, he learned some things he'd never do again. "You're the only show in town," he reminded himself, gathering the lot in a folder. He smoothed his new shirt. "And a very professional show at that." He looked into the mirror.

"Sign them," O'Keeffe insisted.

"The photographs?" he asked. O'Keeffe didn't answer, and Parker realized that it would be good for business to have his name with his work. "Sign them on the back?" he asked.

"Only a fool would do that!" She handed him a pen.

That night at dinner, Parker collected money and raves for his photographs. The Bishops still had not arrived, though, when Merita cleared the soup bowls from the table. "Perhaps they are ill?" Parker asked, sliding their cactus pictures under his plate. The main course had just arrived when Mrs. Bishop rushed into the dining room. "My pearls!" she said. "They're gone from my suitcase!"

Mr. Bishop hurried behind her. "Arthur!" he demanded. "I insist you get to the bottom of this. My money clip has been emptied."

Arthur rose to his feet. He held up both hands as if to shush the irate guests. "We'll get to the bottom of this," he said quietly. "Could we speak in my office?" When the Bishops did not move, he suggested, "Perhaps your things are just misplaced?"

"How dare you?" Mrs. Bishop hissed. "Don't you think we'd *look* for my precious pearls before we came out here?" Her lower lip quivered

"There, there." Mr. Bishop put an arm around her and glared at Arthur. "There is a thief here. Somebody who knows we would be packing. Somebody new to the ranch, perhaps?" His voice dropped. "Somebody with a criminal history?"

He looked right at Parker. *A criminal record?* A flush crept up Parker's face. He felt the heat of it and knew it made him look guilty. He glanced at O'Keeffe, but the artist refused to meet his eyes.

"I'm sure we can't just go making accusations," Arthur said. "I will have a ranch hand ride down to fetch the sheriff, first thing in the morning." He looked at Mr. Bishop's angry face and added, "Or perhaps I could spare someone now." Arthur turned to leave. "I suggest you all enjoy your suppers. Don't leave the ranch tonight." He looked at O'Keeffe. "Even you, my dear."

"That's O'Keeffe to you," she said, and chuckled. Her laughter fell flat in the silence of the dining room.

"You might as well finish developing today's negatives," O'Keeffe said as they got back to the casita.

"Is anyone going to buy them now?" Parker asked.

"Why ever not?" O'Keeffe shrugged.

"I'm the chief suspect," Parker said. "A proven thief with no alibi. I was in almost everyone's rooms today or yesterday. I was in every building, and I had a camera case over my shoulder. Perfect for hiding necklaces."

"You'll look delightful in all those pearls," O'Keeffe said.

"Don't tease about this," Parker pleaded. "I'm nobody, remember. I'm a drifter. No past and no future. Everybody knows drifters will steal anything they can to stay alive."

"You are *not* a drifter now," O'Keeffe said. "You are an artist."

Parker hooted with scorn. "I'll be in my bedroom when Sheriff Young comes," he said, and slammed the door behind him.

CHAPTER EIGHTEEN

Follow Me

"Follow me," Sheriff Young said.

"Yes, sir," Parker walked into the kitchen, blinking. The electric lightbulb hanging from the ceiling cast a garish glow over the kitchen and reflected rows of shiny photographs. "They turned the generator on again," Parker said, "all in my honor?"

"You have something to confess, son?" the sheriff asked, sitting down in a chair.

Parker wished he had not called him son. He sat down across from the sheriff. "No, sir," he said evenly, just for the record. "I didn't take pearls or anything else."

"Prove it."

Parker sagged. "So you think I did it, like everybody else?"

"What would I think you did?"

"Seems I'd have lifted something from most everybody, sir. Money, jewelry."

"Guns?" the sheriff prompted.

"Sure," Parker said, "why not? Guns, too." He took a breath. "And it had to be me, didn't it, a no-account drifter."

"Whose only source of support," the sheriff said, "was due to leave in a few days."

Parker looked quickly at O'Keeffe. She nodded, then shrugged and said, "Summer's over. I have to go back to New York."

Parker took a long ragged breath. O'Keeffe was leaving him? "It figures," he said. Pain stabbed at his stomach. "You could have told me," he whispered. His mind raced. It was over—again. Where was he supposed to live now? How would he get food? Not the road, he thought. He remembered the hunger, endless hunger. He remembered blisters, and bullies, and beatings. Anything would be better than that.

"Sheriff Young," Parker said quietly. "You're right. I did it." He held out his hands, wrists together, and waited for handcuffs.

"Sorry, son," the sheriff said. "I'm not buying it."

"Look in my camera case," Parker said. The adults stared at him. "Look," he urged. O'Keeffe crossed the room, brought back the case, and handed it to Sheriff Young. "Open it," Parker demanded.

"What's in it?" O'Keeffe asked.

"I'll bet he doesn't know," the sheriff said. "Just like he didn't know you were leaving. Parker here had no reason to take anything." He rocked back on his chair and looked at Parker. "From what I hear, you earned a bundle tonight, fair and square, with your photographs."

"Using equipment I don't own," Parker said. "Except for a camera from a woman I can't trust anymore." Beside him, O'Keeffe gasped. "A woman who would leave without telling me."

"What *is* in here?" Sheriff Young shook the case. Parker thought about refusing to answer, but the sheriff wasn't believing him now, and that would never convince him. O'Keeffe was leaving. He would have to hit the road. If he could prove he was the thief, Parker told himself, he could go with this Sheriff Young, who had four boys of his own and a jail with a stove and a blanket. It got cold in the high desert, he'd heard. Parker took a deep breath. "That's where I put the pearls," he guessed, hoping he sounded certain, hoping he was right.

The sheriff reached in and slowly pulled out a wad of money. "Mr. Bishop's?" O'Keeffe asked.

"Or from one of the other burglaries from this week," the sheriff said, "but there's more." He pulled out a revolver.

"Let me see that," Parker said.

"You know whose it is?" the sheriff asked, ejecting the bullets. Parker held the gun in his hands and stared at it. "Uh, I think so," he said. "But there's no way to know for sure, is there?"

"Not unless we get a confession," the sheriff said, then added, "One I can believe."

"One a jury can see as proof," O'Keeffe said.

Everyone stared at the gun in silence for a moment. "What if I got proof on paper?" Parker finally asked.

"You're not thinking of anything dangerous, Parker, are you?" O'Keeffe asked.

"You're not even going to be here."

"Oh, Parker." O'Keeffe sounded wounded.

"Neither am I," Parker said. "None of us would be in danger—but, for my plan to work, we'd all need to be busy somewhere else tomorrow morning."

"I don't know what lamebrained scheme you've got going," the sheriff said, "but I do have to be here at the ranch anyhow, interviewing everyone. I could stay clear of this casita for most of the day."

"I was planning to paint one last mountain this summer," O'Keeffe said. "Now, with the flowers all about, it would have a different feel, and a different palette, and . . ." She looked at the two of them and finished with, "I'll be out of the way."

"I want to go and rephotograph Clara," Parker said. "Down at her pueblo near Santa Fe." He paused. "In all this mess"—he gestured at the forest of negatives and drifts of prints on the counter—"I think I lost one shot I really liked. May I take your car to the pueblo?"

"Yes," she said. "And Parker, I—"

"Sheriff Young." Parker turned abruptly to the lawman. "I will set things up here tonight. I don't need help anymore."

"Of course," the sheriff said. "You have the most at stake here, clearing your good name."

"*My good name?*" Parker laughed aloud. "Everybody hereabouts knows I stole O'Keeffe's camera. And that I was her 'boy' for a month until she up and snuck home on me."

"Easy, boy," Sheriff Young said.

"Let me do this my way," Parker said. "I think I can have evidence for you—something that a jury will believe—by tomorrow night."

"Follow me," Clara said the next morning, "and do not go into any of these houses alone." As always, she seemed calm. So did her village. It was silent, too, now that the Model A was parked in the shadow of a nearby butte.

Parker studied the tidy row of two- and three-story adobe houses that made up the pueblo. Some had doors, a few had windows, but
the entrance to most was simply a ladder extending from a hole in the
flat roof. Adobe ovens leaked the smells of fresh bread baking and
hot mutton stew. Parker's mouth watered.

"Most everyone is living out at their summer homes now," Clara
said. "They'll all come back for the green corn dance in a few days,
but you should see the village in the winter!" Parker tried to imagine
the high desert with snow and each pueblo with a snowy white
roof and plume of warm smoke. These homes would be cozy. Clara
led him to an older woman singing quietly as she worked in the
sunshine. Parker blinked. The tune was strange and the words were
all wrong, the woman was dark and dressed in pueblo clothing, but
he could not help thinking of his own mother, singing hymns as she
did her housework.

"Mama?" Clara waited until the woman looked up. "This is the
boy I told you about. The one who sees the shepherd in the desert."

"Right pleased to meet you, ma'am," Parker said. As the woman
eyed him suspiciously, he stumbled about, desperate to make a good
impression. "You must be proud of your children, ma'am," he said.
"Clara's pottery is magnificent. And William—"

"Parker is taking pictures of the pueblo," Clara interrupted him,
"with respect. We will not keep you from the work any longer."

"May I snap your picture, ma'am?" Parker asked. At least he
could have a photograph of a mother at work. Clara's mama nodded
and went back to grinding down old pottery shards. "Why is she
doing that?" Parker whispered to Clara.

"Old clay can be wet again and formed into a new bowl," she said. "Even we do not know how many times some of our clay has been used." Parker looked at the woman's strong hands through the viewfinder as they gripped the grindstone. Shards of delicately painted pottery lay in the newly ground dust. Parker snapped a picture of hands making dust into art. Dust that was not making a mother cough. He watched through the viewfinder until Clara touched his elbow.

Then he went around Clara's mother to photograph her back, patiently hunched over her art. There were other pictures he wanted to keep, too, of pueblos carrying bundles of sticks or weaving colorful sashes of wool. He snapped the camera at young children watching, wide eyed, as the adults went about their work. Other children were pretending to do grown-up jobs. Several little ones toddled after Parker, staring into his face or pointing at his hair. He turned, squatted, and took their pictures, too, those who had turned suddenly shy, and those who stood fearless.

Parker rose to his feet and took a long, deep breath. Clara waited silently beside him. "This place is so . . . peaceful." He struggled to find a way to describe his reaction, "And clean and, um, safe."

"And so it has been for thousands of years," Clara said.

Parker looked around at the orderly pueblo. Longing settled thick in his chest. "Clara?" He struggled with the words. "Can anyone stay here?" he asked. "Could I?" Suddenly it made perfect sense to Parker. The tribe could adopt him. Clara was like a sister already. Her mother was here, cooking suppers every day. Clara's father was somewhere nearby, he was sure. Parker's mind raced ahead. He would have a brother, too, in this family, and he could learn to herd sheep. He already knew cattle. Sheep had to be easier. "Clara?"

"It has not been done," she said slowly, "even for those in great need."

Parker stepped back, feeling his face flush with anger. "I'm not in need," he said. "Why, I was just offering to stay here to . . ." He paused. "To help your ma and you for a few weeks until I left."

"You're leaving?" Clara sounded stunned. Parker nodded curtly. "Yep," he said. "There's nothing for me here."

"But where are you going?" Clara asked.

Parker thought quickly. "California. My pa is there. Somewhere."

"You do not believe that."

It was a statement, and the truth of it hit Parker in the gut. "What's that?" he hurled back. "Something your crazy Indian spirit told you? I can't wait to get out of this whole spooky place."

"It was no spirit, Parker," Clara called at his retreating back. "The truth was in your voice."

Parker stormed toward the Model A. "Get away!" he yelled at the pueblo children.

He slammed the car door and hurtled down the road. As he skidded in the soft dirt around a bend, he thought about Clyde's driving and slowed down. But that made him think of Clyde and the ranch and the trap he'd left there. He looked at the sun. It was well past noon: almost time to go back to O'Keeffe's casita. He turned off toward the dry riverbed, wondered if he would ever go back to the Ghost Ranch after this.

The riverbed was full of water, brown and frothy. Parker pulled the Model A to a stop. The water bubbled and chortled over stones—round ones that O'Keeffe liked to collect. Parker shook his head to clear that thought, but over the rushing sound of the water, it seemed he could hear her voice.

"Parker." The voice was coming from behind him, and it *was* O'Keeffe. Parker slouched low in his seat and waited.

The artist opened the passenger door, got in, and closed it. "Parker. Listen to me." Parker stared through the windshield at the rushing water. "I was going to tell you about leaving."

"Yes, ma'am," he grumbled. "I'm sure you were."

"*And,* I was going to ask you to travel back to New York City with me."

So she thought he was in great need, too? "So now I'm supposed to think you are really kind?"

"No, I'm not, and we both know it." She paused. "I always drive to and from New Mexico and I always find a victim to go with me, to share the driving and keep me sane."

Parker waited.

"You'd see the whole country," she said. "I have no set plan for the route. We could even stop by your old home."

"No!" Parker's vehemence startled them both.

"Fine, then. But you could see the Mississippi. And the Shenandoah Mountains. And the Capitol. Lake George and New York City."

"What am I supposed to do if I follow you there?" Parker finally spoke. "I don't know anyone in New York."

"You'll know me, and I can introduce you around. You'll like Alfred."

"I doubt it," Parker muttered.

"Worst come to worst, I'll buy you a train ticket to get you back home. Wherever that is."

Parker winced. "I'll think about it."

"Then it's done," O'Keeffe said firmly. "Let me get my paints and we can drive back to the ranch."

Parker drove, but the desert slid past the Model A's windows unnoticed. The Mississippi? Washington, D.C.? Nobody he knew back home had ever been there—or even out of the county. Those were not real places, yet he could go—if he could bear to sit in the same car with O'Keeffe for that long. She sat silent beside him. Parker glanced at her and wondered what other secrets she might be keeping.

CHAPTER NINETEEN

Clyde

As Parker drove up to the casita, he had to swerve around Clyde. The ranch hand jerked the Model A's door open before the engine died. "Did you see Merita?" he demanded, leaning into the car. Parker smelled whiskey, sweat, and something else—fear?

"What's the matter?" Parker packed his voice with sarcasm. "Your girlfriend find out about you?"

"Calm down, both of you," O'Keeffe said. "Is something wrong, Clyde?"

Parker was amazed at how cool O'Keeffe was playing it.

"She's gone. Cleaned me out and left." Clyde sounded near tears. "Where's Uncle Arthur?"

"*Uncle* Arthur?" Parker repeated. "Mr. Pack is your uncle?"

"We haven't seen either of them," O'Keeffe said.

"I have to find them!" The Model A rocked as Clyde pushed his body away and ran off toward the main house.

"My, my," O'Keeffe said, getting out of the automobile.

"Clyde and Arthur are related?" Parker asked. He thought about all of Arthur's money. Clyde was rich?

"I thought you knew." O'Keeffe grabbed her sketch pad. "When the boy's parents divorced, he went wild. Stupid things: law trouble, girl trouble, you name it." She pointed to her chalk case and Parker picked it up for her. "Nobody in the family would have Clyde, except Arthur."

"Why would Arthur take him in?"

"Some of us have a fondness for young'uns with spirit," O'Keeffe said.

"I'm not like Clyde."

"'Course not. Didn't say you were. Can we go in now?"

The casita door was standing open. "Oh, no!" O'Keeffe said, looking at the brushes scattered across the floor by Parker's new camera case. He didn't need to look to know it was empty. Instead, he looked up. Half of the strings full of negatives were torn down. "Good," he said.

"Good?" O'Keeffe's voice was shrill. "Good? I'll have to get that Merita in here pronto to clean up this mess!"

Parker was pulling a sheet off the old camera he'd tucked onto the corner of the counter. He unhooked the string from its shutter and grinned. "I have some developing to do."

"That was the trap?"

"Yup," Parker said. "When Clyde tried to get his gun"—he gestured to the case on the floor in a tangle of string—"he took his own picture." O'Keeffe glanced at all of her brushes. "Oh, I wired those in, too. The clatter of them hitting the ground covered the sound of the shutter. That's why Clyde still doesn't know we have him on film!"

"But he has the gun!" she said.

"He doesn't know it's empty."

"You'd better develop that film." O'Keeffe put the last of the brushes back into their jar. "I have a lot of packing to do, so I'll be out of your way."

"You're not staying for the powwow?"

"I've seen it before. Too many people crammed into the pueblo for my taste. Tourists."

"Tourists like us," Parker said. He thought of the peace of the Indian village. Clara had been right. They did not need others there. Others like him. He turned to the camera and barely noticed as O'Keeffe eased the door shut.

When Parker held up the negative, dripping, he knew he had a problem. The focus was off and the lighting, too. "I can't make anything of this," he called to O'Keeffe.

"Print it," she said. "Sometimes it is hard to tell what you have until you see what develops."

Hours later, as he stared at the print, he was glad the electricity was on for the second night. The door opened. "O'Keeffe?" he called.

"I brought you some food," she said. "It was quiet tonight in the dining room, and slow." She set a paper bag on the table and the rich smell of roast lamb filled the kitchen. "They were short handed."

"Look at this," Parker said.

O'Keeffe stared at the muddy photograph. "I can't make much of it. Except for this." She pointed to a cross that had caught the light at just the right moment. "It's a fancy one. Do you know any-body who wears a necklace like this?"

"I do. And it isn't Clyde."

"Do tell."

"Merita," Parker said slowly. "Merita who loves adventure. And jewelry. Who sees all these wealthy women around her—"

"—and has nothing of her own." O'Keeffe finished his thought.

"Except for a boyfriend she couldn't talk into robbing banks."

"Do you think that's where she is? Out robbing banks?"

Parker shrugged. "Maybe. Clyde was here twice while you were gone, asking if I'd seen her." He shook his head. "Sad."

"You've been doing a lot of thinking?"

Parker simply nodded.

"Do you want to go out and do evening rounds by yourself?" O'Keeffe suggested. "I'll stay here in case Sheriff Young comes by."

"Yes, please. I have someone to talk to before I start packing."

The bleating of sheep led Parker to William. "They are restless tonight," William explained.

"Do they sense a big cat out there?"

"I think they are feeling a change coming in the seasons."

Parker stood next to the Indian and looked out toward the Sangre de Cristos. The boys watched together as the sunset painted the mountaintops a strange rose color and, one by one, the sheep bedded down along the slope below them. "Would you like some water?" Parker finally offered. "I brought some supper, too. O'Keeffe fixed it up for me tonight. There's enough for two."

"She is generous," William said, sitting down on a wide flat rock.

"O'Keeffe would argue with you on that one. She doesn't always say what you'd expect."

"Maybe she doesn't see what is clear to everyone else."

"That's like Clyde," Parker said, handing William some meat. "He really believed that Merita loved him."

"The pueblo people have a saying: 'Men in search of a myth will usually find one.'"

Parker thought about that while William thanked the sheep for giving him food. "That finding-a-myth-you-need thing," Parker said. "That's true for art, too, isn't it? People see what they want in O'Keeffe's paintings." He noticed one star glimmering near the horizon, then another overhead. "I saw an Indian rain spirit in Clara's bowl," Parker said. "I even had myself believing it brought that cloudburst."

A sheep down the hill bleated softly and went back to sleep. The two boys were licking their fingers before William spoke again. "You are leaving."

"Now that *is* spooky," Parker said. "How did you know?"

"You are restless and talking faster. You keep looking at the sky and the desert as though you already miss them."

"You didn't use some Indian magic to read my mind, then?" Parker said.

"No. Must you go before the corn dance?" When Parker nodded, William sighed. "That is a shame. But have you said good-bye to Clara as you have to me?"

Parker was silent.

"You must," William said, "just as you must now go back to the ranch and finish things there."

Parker extended his hand. "Thank you, William. You were there when I needed you in the desert, and I'll never forget you."

William stood, starlight glinting in his dark eyes, and shook hands with Parker. The same bright starlight lit Parker's way back to the Ghost Ranch. It showed pale on the sheriff's car in the driveway of O'Keeffe's casita.

"Glad you're back, Parker, my boy," Sheriff Young said from a kitchen chair. He took a swallow from a cup as O'Keeffe hovered nearby with a teapot. "I thought you ought to know, I've given out your old room at the jail to a young lady."

"Merita?"

"Yes, Merita with the taste for money and jewels. She claims it is all Clyde's doing, but I doubt that."

"Why?" Parker asked. He took the cup O'Keeffe was offering.

"Oh, Clyde's angry, all right. The boy talks a mean game and plays wicked jokes on tenderfeet hereabouts, but he's all bluster. It's the anger that a jury would hear, though Clyde is settling down some. I just wish I could show them some proof. . . ."

Parker set down his cup and pulled the day's photograph from the drying screen. "This might help." The sheriff peered at it, turned it sideways, and looked back at Parker. "That fancy cross," Parker explained. "You'll see it on Merita's neck."

The sheriff nodded. "I saw it when we made her take it off—and sealed it in an evidence envelope." He grinned. "Good work!" The sheriff took another sip of tea. "Now, O'Keeffe tells me you are thinking of leaving with her. Am I right?"

"After I make one last visit to Santo Domingo Pueblo," Parker said.

"I was thinking that you could stay on with me and the missus," the sheriff said, "iff'n you wanted to. Pret' near asked you back when you were my guest, but I guess O'Keeffe here made you an offer I couldn't top."

Parker drew in his breath. "O'Keeffe?" He looked at the artist.

She shrugged and gestured toward the sheriff.

"Can I take you up on that, sheriff," Parker asked, his eyes locked with O'Keeffe's, "if I happen to come back this way, say, by train, in a few weeks?" He watched O'Keeffe's face relax and her eyes fill.

"What are you wasting time for," she scolded, "just standing there drinking tea? We have got a load of packing to do!"

"Clara," Parker said the next morning.

The girl looked up from the mutton she was cutting on a flat board on her lap. "Parker!" She scraped the meat into a great kettle. "Are you coming to the green corn ceremony?"

"No. But I had to come and say good-bye."

"You are leaving with O'Keeffe, then?"

"I am going to live with her and her husband, Alfred. They are both famous artists, you know. In New York City, thousands of miles from here."

"Did you come back to tell me that?" Clara asked. She reached for a handful of green chilies.

"No," Parker admitted. "William reminded me to say good-bye to you."

"William?" Clara's knife hung in the air over the chilies.

"Yes, last night, with his sheep out under the stars." He pictured it again. "Thousands of stars."

"Parker." Clara's voice shook. "There *is* no William. He is only a spirit in the desert. The spirit of a shepherd who comes to help—sometimes."

Parker was silent. No William? "But . . . I *saw* him, Clara. Like I saw the rain-bringer deer. Soi'ngwa?" He stumbled about, trying to make sense of her words.

"Soi'ngwa is a real spirit, Parker, as real as this village. He has always been here for us, bringing the rain that keeps us alive."

"Don't sheep keep you alive?" Parker pointed at the cook pot.

Clara shook her head. "Sheep are as new here as the white men. So are shepherds. You saw a spirit, Parker. They are everywhere, in the desert, in rocks and mountains . . ."

". . . in skulls, and skull paintings, and in your painted bowls, too." He thought of Alfred Stieglitz's pictures. "Even in photographs." He cleared his throat and shook his head. "No, Clara. An Indian—or a superstitious person—could believe all this. It's just too spooky for me."

"Take the memory with you, Parker, all those thousands of miles," Clara said. "You are one of the lucky ones. I am honored to have known you."

Parker watched her walk back to help her mother prepare for the green corn ceremony.

CHAPTER TWENTY

The Show

Three weeks, two thousand miles, and one flat tire later, Parker and
O'Keeffe arrived in New York. Mounting a major art show takes
months, and O'Keeffe was not ready for hers until January. In all that
time, Parker never got used to the city. There was no room to walk
alone; no quiet place to think. The streets were narrow little canyons;
sunless, dirty, and choked with noise. Even the parks were cluttered
with trees and, like everywhere else, full of strangers. The sky stayed
trapped away behind huge buildings, peeking through only as stripes
of blue or a starless black at night.

O'Keeffe's city paintings showed that she felt the same way about
the place, but she wouldn't talk with him about it. Neither would her
husband, Alfred Stieglitz. The photographer was even more distant
than O'Keeffe and prickly as barbed wire. They fought, too, worse
than Parker's parents ever had. He counted the days until the art
show opening. Parker hoped everyone would relax after that and he
could begin to fit in.

🙟 🙟 🙟

Parker stood stiffly in new clothes: pants that were not jeans, short boots that had no holes in the bottoms, and a white shirt with a bow tie. His mouth was stiff and his teeth seemed to be drying out. He had smiled first at seeing O'Keeffe's paintings hung in the empty studio. It was like seeing old friends in this dark, crowded city. The melted mountains were there and the flowers, Clara's kachinas and the goat's skull. Goose bumps had crept along Parker's arms as he felt the skull stare at him from the canvas. Finally he turned to the other paintings. There were thirty-six of them in all.

Parker grinned to find a picture of the ram's skull in the printed catalog. It, too, stared at him, as bleak and strong and alive as the desert itself. Parker smiled politely at O'Keeffe's fans, who had rushed into An American Place, Alfred Stieglitz's new Manhattan art studio, as soon as its doors opened. He gave a wide smile to O'Keeffe, who was doing her best act, making everyone laugh uproariously around her. He grinned at everyone he met. "Remember their names," O'Keeffe had hissed at him. He was almost expecting a quiz that night, but things were so different here.

Parker tried to relax and joke with Stieglitz and the men he introduced. Stieglitz was a genius as a photographer but he was old and short. O'Keeffe clearly loved him. So did handfuls of his students, men whom he'd helped to become famous photographers. But Parker was not impressed. Whenever Parker and O'Keeffe began to talk, Stieglitz butted in, interrupting and steering the conversation—and often O'Keeffe—away.

Tonight, Parker carefully smiled at Stieglitz. He smiled until he thought his lips would crack, and then he glanced at O'Keeffe and felt a real smile begin again. She deserved this, he thought, and every fan she had.

"Is this the young man?" a dark-coated dandy asked Stieglitz.

"Yes, yes," the photographer said. "Did you bring his portfolio?"

The man sniffed and said, "Of course I did, and he's as gifted as you said."

"Then I'll leave you two to discuss business," Stieglitz said, and rushed to O'Keeffe's side.

"Mr. Ray?" the man said. "May I call you Parker?" He didn't wait for an answer. "I'm Hank Martin, Parker, my boy. We need to find a table to look at your work."

"My work?"

"Oh, ho, ho! Isn't that just like Stieglitz! Delightful!" He studied Parker. "I thought you were older." Parker could feel his stiff smile dying.

"What is this about, Mr. Martin?" he demanded.

In answer, the fancy-dressed man slapped a big book onto a table and gestured at a chair. Parker sat down, opened the book, and stopped short. Clara's face filled the first page, calm, alert, and intelligent. Parker flipped through pages of his photographs from New Mexico. There were the bat and the mountains, windmill blades against the sky, the eagle flying over Sheriff Young's hat, the peace of the square at the pueblo, and finally, Clara's mother, looking ancient as she ground old pots into new.

Parker felt his neck flush and then his cheeks. "How dare he?" he hissed. "These are mine!"

"Everyone knows that," Hank said. "And it is a wonderful portfolio, just wonderful."

"What did he say?" O'Keeffe leaned over the table, her eyes
sparkling.

"I haven't told him yet."

Parker held the book to his chest and shifted in his seat.

"Well, Mr. Ray," Hank gushed. "The WPA wants you!" Parker
looked at O'Keeffe. She looked thrilled. Alfred had come to the table
to hear his reaction, too.

"I don't know what you are talking about!" Parker said. "I don't
know what you are saying and I don't know what you want *me* to
say." He glanced desperately around the room. It was so crowded
with people that there seemed no room to breathe. They were all
dressed up and talking fast, and they all belonged here in the city.
Parker suddenly knew that he did not fit here—and never would. He
looked toward the door and ached for sky, a big blue sky.

"Parker." O'Keeffe's hand was on his shoulder. "Relax and listen.
You remember hearing about the CCC, right?" Parker nodded, slowly. That was the government plan to hire men to work in state parks.
"The WPA," O'Keeffe explained, "is Roosevelt's plan for artists of
all kinds who can't make a living with the economy so bad."

"Writers are taking down the words of ex-slaves," Stieglitz said.
"Songwriters are recording old folk songs from the mountains, sculp-
tors are designing monuments, that sort of thing."

"And they are making a living at it," O'Keeffe said.

"I owe everything I know to Stieglitz," Hank said, glancing at his
old teacher. "Now I am a photographer documenting the new bridges

being built all over the country. And I am also in charge of screening new photographers for the Works Projects Administration."

"The WPA," O'Keeffe whispered. "Parker, I know you are upset,"—she put her hand over his on the cover of the portfolio—"but by sending the best of your work back here for Alfred to package like this, I thought I could help you. I just never imagined what our circle of contacts—and your talent—could do for you."

The conversation paused while a magazine photographer took a picture of her in Stieglitz's arms by the mountain painting. Then she came back. "Did you tell him the best part yet?" she asked Hank.

"On the basis of this portfolio, Parker, you've been selected to document the effects of the Dust Bowl."

"What does that mean?" Parker asked, feeling his heart rate soar.

"That means," O'Keeffe explained, "they want you to drive through the country, making photographs of people like your own family, historic pictures that will capture the spirit of our times."

"Can I take pictures in Indian country, too?"

Hank nodded. "It also means that you would have to pack quickly. We can have you on an airplane to Washington, D.C., tonight."

Parker glanced at the ram's skull painting and smiled.

Georgia O'Keeffe's Life and Art

Georgia O'Keeffe's talent was first recognized by her farm wife mother, who managed to get her to weekly art lessons in Sun Prairie, Wisconsin. Two of O'Keeffe's sisters were also talented, but none was as driven as Georgia, who attended art school in Chicago. She studied under the famous painter William Merritt Chase, who taught a very traditional style and method of painting where realism was the highest form of art. She learned to draw exactly what she saw, rendering accurately.

After a few years spent teaching and painting in this style, O'Keeffe studied at Columbia University in New York City with Arthur Wesley Dow. He valued design and experimental approaches to painting. "Fill a space," he said. "And fill it beautifully."

O'Keeffe often visited 291 in New York, a gallery owned by the radical photographer Alfred Stieglitz. The gallery specialized in new styles of art, showing the work of Pablo Picasso, Auguste Rodin, Henri Matisse, Marsden Hartley, and other painters as well as innovative photographers. There was nothing traditional about these "modern artists."

Stricken by the contrast between her own student-level work and these creative geniuses, O'Keeffe quit painting altogether. Still, within a few years, her talent bubbled up again. Out on the wild Texas plains where she was teaching, she imagined a series of shapes and then drew them boldly in charcoal on paper. A friend to whom she had sent them showed the drawings to Stieglitz, who recognized their genius and put them in a show at 291.

O'Keeffe demanded that Stieglitz take them down. He refused. Stieglitz was drawn to this gangly, opinionated young painter and decided to champion her career as he had so many others. That business relationship quickly deepened into love and, finally, to a long-distance marriage. While O'Keeffe needed space, both personal and emotional, Stieglitz wanted control. Throughout her married life, Georgia left her husband at home so she could paint in new places where she felt free and inspired.

Before she discovered the West, O'Keeffe found flowers as a motif in her art. She painted them huge, often on enormous canvases, so that the viewer would have the same overwhelming experience she did as she studied the blossoms. These bold abstracts were so different and so riveting that they caused a stir in the art world—and the press. Many called them thinly veiled erotic pictures. Stieglitz said nothing to correct that impression, for it helped to make O'Keeffe more famous.

When O'Keeffe's younger sister began painting enormous flowers, too, selling them as "O'Keeffe paintings," Georgia began looking for a new subject and more space. She found both in New Mexico. First the desert hills and the lonely churches, then the skulls and landscapes filled her canvases. Her fame was worldwide.

By the time of Stieglitz's death in 1946, the art world was shifting. No longer were abstractions such as O'Keeffe's in style. Now the nonobjective art of Jackson Pollock and William de Kooning were in fashion. Georgia began traveling the world. Still she painted. Some of her works were intimate abstractions of courtyards and doorways. Other enormous paintings showed the vast cloudscapes and sky-scapes she saw through airplane windows.

While she remained vigorous to the end of her life, O'Keeffe's eyesight failed. In 1972, when a handsome young potter stopped by to ask for any odd jobs, she hired him on the spot. For the next twenty-five years, he worked with her, managing O'Keeffe's busi-ness as her paintings swung back into style, teaching her to make pottery as her irrepressible talent bubbled up again, aiding her as her health declined, and most of all being a friend. She left him all of her paintings and belongings when she died. She left us with a glimpse of the beauty she saw in flowers, the West, and the world—and a way to catch the spirit beneath the surfaces we see.

A Timeline of O'Keeffe's Life

November 15, 1887   Georgia O'Keeffe born on large dairy farm outside of Sun Prairie, Wisconsin.

1903   Moves to Virginia. By eighth grade announces, "I will become an artist."

1905   Graduates high school, attends the Art Institute of Chicago.

1907   Enters the Art Students League in New York City. Wins scholarship for traditional painting of dead rabbit.

1908   Stops painting, frustrated with limits of realistic art.

1912–1918   Teaches in Amarillo, Texas, the University of Virginia, Teachers College at Columbia University in New York City, and Texas State Normal College.

1916   A friend brings O'Keeffe's black-and-white nonobjective drawings to Alfred Stieglitz, who exhibits them at his famous 291 studio in New York.

1917   Another show at 291 includes watercolors from Texas.

1918   Leaves Texas and moves to New York City to live with Stieglitz, twenty-four years her senior. Spends summers at Lake George, winters in Manhattan.

1924   Marries Stieglitz. Paints first of her huge flower paintings.

1929   Takes train trip to Taos, New Mexico, and falls in love with desert area; learns to drive. Summers in New Mexico instead of Lake George.

1930   Paints first of her "bone" paintings.

1934   Visits posh Ghost Ranch in Abiquiu, New Mexico; decides to return yearly.

1935   Paints kachinas, *Ram's Skull with Brown Leaves.*

1940   Buys home on Ghost Ranch property.

1945   Buys abandoned hacienda in Abiquiu, near Ghost Ranch. Begins restoring it.

1946   Stieglitz has stroke and dies. O'Keeffe settles estate over next three years.

1955   Arthur Pack gives the Ghost Ranch to the Presbyterian Church as a retreat and educational site.

1961   O'Keeffe takes seventeen-day rafting trip down Colorado River at seventy-four years old. Begins painting series of smooth black rocks. Begins painting skyscapes as seen from airplane windows.

1962   Is elected to the fifty-member American Academy of Arts and Letters. Has a major retrospective at the Whitney Museum, in New York City.

1972   Stops painting as eyesight fails.

1973   Juan Hamilton, a handsome young potter, becomes her companion, business manager, pottery instructor.

1976   Writes book with Hamilton about her art and allows video production.

1984   Moves into Hamilton's house in Sante Fe to be near medical facilities.

1986   Dies at ninety-eight; her ashes scattered the next day over her favorite desert mountaintop.

FOR MORE INFORMATION

Readers can learn more about Georgia O'Keeffe's life from:

Georgia O'Keeffe: Painter, by Michael L. Berry (Women of Achievement series, Chelsea House, Broomall, PA, 2003)

Georgia O'Keeffe: Legendary American Painter, by Jodie A. Shull (Enslow Publishers, Berkeley Heights, NJ, 2003).

For a lavishly illustrated biography and analysis of O'Keeffe's art, see *Georgia O'Keeffe,* by Lisa Mintz Messinger (Thames & Hudson, Inc., London and New York, 2001).

Far longer, *Portrait of an Artist, A Biography of Georgia O'Keeffe,* by Laurie Lisle (Simon & Schuster, New York, NY, 1980 and 1986) looks at O'Keeffe's life in fascinating detail.

The Georgia O'Keeffe Museum in Sante Fe, New Mexico, exhibits the actual ram's skull along with many famous O'Keeffe paintings and Albert Stieglitz photographs. Visit its web site at okeeffemuseum.org/index.php.

Ram's Skull with Brown Leaves hangs in the Roswell Museum and Art Center in Roswell, New Mexico. View the painting on the web at www.roswellmuseum.org.

Look for the teacher's guide to *The Spirit Catchers* on the Web.

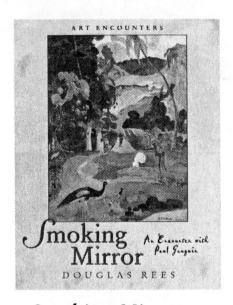

Smoking Mirror:
An Encounter with Paul Gauguin
by Douglas Rees

The White Wolf killed his best friend. Now Joe Sloan seeks revenge. As he navigates the unknown territory of 1891 Tahiti and its people, he finds an unlikely ally in the French artist, Paul Gauguin.

REVIEWS FOR AUTHOR DOUGLAS REES:

"Rees lights the story with flashes of lyricism . . . In much of historical fiction, the answers have to be fabricated; here, Rees trusts readers to ponder the excitement of the questions themselves."
—*Kirkus Reviews* on *Lightning Time*

". . . historically accurate, richly detailed."—*School Library Journal* on *Lightning Time*

". . . the story is fluid and fun."—*Publishers Weekly* on *Vampire High*

Hardcover ISBN: 0-8230-4863-2
Price: $15.95